The magic of Cloud Cottage

By Carol Savage

About the Author

Born in Radford, Carol has lived most of her life in Nottingham. Married to an American, they ran a pet shop for 35 years and Carol slotted writing poetry, film scripts and now this book between bringing up three children and working in the shop. She is a feminist and feels strongly about the unfairness, suffering and injustice of gender inequality. She also loves being outdoors and nature is also paramount in her writing.

A word from the Author

My aim within this story is to actually show domestic abuse in action. There are, of course, many aspects to this perverse behaviour and I hope by telling the story of Cloud Cottage, by giving an example, it may create an understanding of how damaging domestic violence is to not just partners but children, families, friendships, the workplace, communities and countries.

This book is published by William Savage Publishing, first edition in Nottingham, United Kingdom, 2024.

Art cover and book design by Bárbara Orellana-Becerra, Kió Studio Design, United Kingdom

ISBN 978-1-0686454-0-2

Carol Savage

The magic of Cloud Cottage

With many Thanks for
supporting
Broxtowe Women's Project –
Carol Savage.

To Stuart, Sally and Joe.

Content

Friday

Meeting up

They all arrived at once. It was chaos. The Hunter family pulled up, their immaculate white Audi skewwiff across the drive, making it difficult for the Morris family to pull their battered old Ford alongside. The contrast between, not only the cars but also the occupants, would be immediately obvious to even the most unobservant of onlookers. The Ford had all its windows wound down, there were flashes of red curls beside black straight hair, glimpses of hippy bright scarves and jackets and a lot of noisy excitement as faces stuck out, calling and waving to the family silently climbing out of the 'posh' car. The driver of the Audi in a tweed country raincoat, the woman in a smart blue suit, gold round her neck, the children, fashionable track suits and top brand trainers. They lined up to stare at the rowdy circus clambering out of the wreck. The face of a dog suddenly appeared, a mass of brown fur and lollopy ears. It took one look at the aloof, squashy face of the Persian cat perched primly in the woman's arms and, barking manically, leap-frogged over the back of the young girl and out of the car window. The cat of course reacted. It doubled in size and suddenly took on the appearance of a toilet brush, its claws sank into its owner, who shrieked loudly, then it leapt to the ground, running furiously towards the nearest tree, the huge brown bear of a dog in pursuit.

'What the fuck' exclaimed Simon, patting down his coat and picking up his now paw-printed suitcase.

'Oh Simon,' murmured Clare as she studied the deep scratches on her arm, 'the kids can hear'.

Tall and graceful for a twelve year old, Celia tumbled over the bags of clothes and boxes of food stacked in the van footwell, then ran over to the other family to kiss each startled face and call out their names.

"Uncle Simon. How are you. It's been so long. Isn't this fun? Auntie Clare those scratches look nasty. Sorry about our dog."

When she loped over to kiss her cousins they both looked horrified.

"You're not kissing me." exclaimed Niall, hurrying to stand beside his father. Bethany glared at Celia.

"Call that mutt off" she yelled , hurrying to the tree to nervously stand a good few feet away from the hysterical dog. The cat stretched himself luxuriously along a branch just out of reach of its crazed adversary and stared smugly down, for all intents the grinning cat in Alice in Wonderland . From the sheltered vantage of the rain drooped branches around her Bethany studied the two families awkwardly facing each other. 'She knew she shouldn't have come. These cousins she was expected to interact with looked like hippies. More than likely they would be suggesting camping in the garden to study the stars or a tramp through muddy fields to look for fossils or something.' She stroked her long hair for comfort then glanced down at her white Nike trainers. They were already scuffed. Her lip pursed. 'The dog was scary. Better to leave it.' Bethany picked her way back to her dad and brother, her face folding into tight lines of disdain to match theirs.

"Why the hell did you bring that dog?" shouted Simon towards the man unfolding out of the old van.

"And 'hello' to you" called Dan. "I could ask why on earth you've brought a CAT!"

He strolled towards his brother in law and stopped a few feet away, dark hair flopping across his eyes and his slim shape a complete contrast to Simon's yellow buzz cut and solid shouldered bulk.

"Now now, Dan." Rosie crossed the path to the two men. "Not a good start eh brother?

She smiled at Simon but fell short of hugging him, instead looping her arm through Dan's. Her black hair glinted red as it swung round her shoulders and she turned to her sister in law. "Hello Clare. How was your journey? "

Clare smiled back at the friendly grin and smiling dark eyes.

"It was fine, thank you Rosie."

Rosie peered towards the posh car. "Did you forget to bring mother?"

A voice called feebly from the back of the Audi. "At last. Someone's actually remembered me. I'm in here. Can somebody kindly help me out, I'm getting very stiff."

"Gran." called Celia and rushed to help.

Her voice came through the door first "Thank you dear. It's just my poor old knees. I thought we'd never get here. There was so much traffic and Simon would not stop to let his mother get a cup of tea". The old ladies bottom emerged first, guided out by Celia's hands each side of the adequate hips, blue pleated skirt billowing in the wind. A wrinkled hand appeared, grabbing at the skirt, her voice still within the car "Hold on to my modesty Celia."

"Keep going gran. You're nearly there." Celia encouraged, winking at her brother.

And blinking round, the old lady was out. "Clare, take me in. I'm so parched."

Clare smiled guiltily at Celia as she took over navigating the elderly galleon. "It is so lovely to see you all. Thank you Celia, I'll just take mother and go and make us all a nice cuppa."

"Look at all these flagstones. Hold on to me dear." Grace leaned heavily on her aide and they staggered wonkily up the path, complaints floating over their shoulders.

Rosie and Dan stepped back as if a royal cavalcade was passing by. Dan doffed an invisible cap.

"If I'd have stopped we'd have had to make a wee stop five minutes down the road." Simon said from behind a tall pile of matching suitcases "We've not moved in here Bethany. It's only for a week." he called to the girl back at the tree, trying to haul the cat down. "If that dog hurts our Squash. He's a very valuable cat." And with that he marched up to the house, trundling three suitcases noisily behind him.

Dan glanced at Rosie. "your brother is rude and your mother didn't even acknowledge you."

Rosie shrugged in a 'What's new' way.

Ewan ran over to the tree to tousle the dogs floppy topknot, she grinned toothily back, tongue flopping crazily down. He shared the same languid frame as his sister but somewhere down the genetic line of ancestors there had been a rogue freckled red head who now re-emerged in this wiry, boisterous boy.

Dan called from the back of the van."Come and grab your bags kids and clear all this detritus off the seats please."

"Right-o dad." The siblings were bouncing across the path when they saw a small red sports car parked behind a shed so dilapidated and shrouded in ivy it was almost invisible. Elgar and cigar smoke drifted lazily out of the car window. Ewan strolled over. "Uncle John. Are you hiding?"

A big framed man hauled his paunch out of the low seat and stood up. He brushed cigar ash and biscuit crumbs from crumpled old trousers before staring at the youngsters as if trying to recall how he knew them. "You're such a noisy lot." Ewan moved to hug his uncle but he sidestepped and strolled past up the path to the house "I hope my room is en-suite and away from your lot's racket" he muttered, as if addressing the droning bees. Then the oak front door slammed behind him.

"Boy, he's got no filter has he?" Celia whispered to her brother.

"And he's just ignored us as well." Dan glanced at Rosie "Just remind me why we've done this!" they were hauling their rucksacks past a drift of orange flowers, they, at least seemed to be nodding a welcome.

"Because mum wanted us all together for once, I've not seen her for ages, we've not had a holiday and she's paid for it, plus it's a beautiful part of the country."

"Fair enough. We'll just have to keep our traps firmly shut. Look at them kids." the parents smiled indulgently as they watched their youngsters picking up all the gunky picnic leftovers, trying to stop them spilling onto their belongings, while swinging rucksacks onto their shoulders. They were laughing as books and clothes tipped onto the gravel, followed by consoles and a walkman as they bent over. Chuckling, the parents hurried over to help. Struggling over the gravel with the bags and a case, Dan stopped in front of the porch to admire the pale oak archway and stained glass windows each side. It was as if they were entering a Hobbit house. He then noticed an inscription burnt into the wood overhead. 'Enter these portals and find courage through Love.'

"Wow. Look at this." was all he could say before taking one last look at the view of fields and hills stretching to the horizon and a setting sun as the Gothic door slammed firmly shut behind them. Dan had the uneasy feeling their family was being shut in a prison.

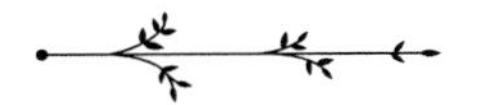

The Cottage

The collective and chaotic arrival did not prevent all members of the Morris family from taking in the beauty of the cottage and surrounding countryside on arrival. It was a balmy late afternoon when the map indicated Cloud Hill but could not prepare them for the rows of whispering lime trees or the leaves drifting onto their bonnets in glorious reds, greens and yellows. Enclosing the huddle of cottages in the valley, soft hills carried their white parcels of clouds and small drifts of mist on a backdrop of vivid blue. Cream mounds of sheep were dotted around hedge squared fields shining emerald, backed by the autumnal dazzle of muscular woods. Sticking their heads out of the windows as the van coughed its way through old rotting wood gates, the family breathed in deeply the crisp, clean air. Only the engine and the rustle and chatter of sparrows in the hedgerow sounded their arrival at Cloud cottage. And what a breathtaking jumble of twisted chimneys, glinting mullioned windows, decayed sheds and lean-tos the old place was. The garden, a riotous carnival of jewelled flowers, bending and swaying, an invitation to admire their beauty. The whole place was at once garish, a fairytale and a breathtaking plunge into a more simple and sensuous rural past.

The family in the Audi in front were silent. The rural pageant through the windows was lost on their urban senses. Clare was considering whether she might get a bit of peace of mind and escape Simon's rule with other people around. Niall, how reliable would the internet be so that he could continue his game of 'Lord of The Rings: Return of the King .' Bethany hoping for a room with en-suite, plenty of hot water and a good internet connection so she could use her new addiction, the mobile phone, an invention still only acquired by the more affluent families. Simon, how far was it to the golf club and pub and would he get in the house first so he could claim the biggest bedroom with the best view. Grace, whether it was possible to get her family to give her every consideration without them falling out. John wondered if he would get away with smoking in the house and how far it was to the nearest pub. But the family in the old van were totally enthralled by the sight, sounds and smells of the countryside. Rosie intrigued at the likelihood of completely different country views than those around their home. Celia and Ewan imagined rocky streams and wellies, muddy paths, hot baths and stews. While Dan dreamt of a tiny library at the top of the house and perfect silence, away from the other family. The dog already loved the country smells and the sight of white, fluffy things moving around in empty fields, being more used to huge lumbering beasts in their corner of the country. Black and white or brown beasts you would be mad to chase as they would stand their ground, possibly even turn on a rowdy, barking dog. And the brown ones even had horns!

Once inside the cottage Rosie's first impression was of a large and cosy old pine kitchen, dark green tiles and Aga, the fur ball of a cat curled in front, vying for heat with Grace. Her frock dangled over him and he showed his displeasure by the rhythmic beating of his tail. Clare was busily opening each cupboard door in search of mugs, the kettle steaming cheerily beside her.

"Look at this. Proper china cups and saucers. Would any of you lot like tea?"

Rosie smiled warmly. "Yes please. Dan and I would love one. Can I leave you to it? I'm desperate for the loo."

"Wow." Rosie whistled to herself as, bladder bursting and bent double, she hauled up the dark oak stairs, noting the glow of orange velvet curtains across huge hall windows. Suddenly a bum was in her sight, travelling fast towards her and straddling the bannister. She grabbed her daughter as she whizzed past and with some effort, hauled Celia off, nearly off balancing them both. "You can pack that up young lady and behave yourself while you're here."

Celia tightened the hug and gave a cheeky response. "I was just doing some speed polishing."

Her mum tried not to laugh. "Just get yourself into that kitchen and say hello to your aunt and gran properly."

Now Rosie had to really rush along the upstairs corridor. As she passed, a glow of sunset reflected on walls of a huge bedroom, a view over the front garden and pink fields beyond glistened through mullioned windows. A movement in the corner revealed Simon fastidiously hanging his clothes in a huge old wardrobe. 'And he's got the only en suite' she thought as she charged into the bathroom, barely having time to slam the door shut and lift the toilet lid.

Meanwhile, an argument was going on next door. Bethany had established herself in the second largest bedroom and was blocking her brother in the doorway. "You're not coming in here. Find your own room." He had thrust his body against the door and was pushing back. "There won't be enough rooms. We're supposed to be sharing."

Another door opened and Ewan's head poked out. Behind him, a wallpaper seascape of blue and white beach huts fronting a motionless blue sea, white bunk beds and green octopus lamps on bedside tables. "You can bunk in here with me and Celia if you want, there's plenty of room." Ewan offered but Niall wordlessly rushed past and back down the stairs. Ewan shrugged and followed behind.

Back in the kitchen, Clare was handing out tea and cake, Celia beside her chattering non stop.

"I don't want that dry old fruit cake." Grace called across. "Isn't there any battenburg?"

Duly delivering the cake, Celia stood in front of her gran. "We've not seen you for quite a while. How are you gran?" The old lady stared the girl up and down, noting the vibrant features and wild hair matching her own daughter's and felt a slam of sadness and remorse. But all she said was 'You've grown.' Celia stroked down the wispy grey hair as suddenly Rosie was beside them, face questioning and body hesitant. "Hello mum. How are you?" She leaned forward to clumsily hug her mother, brushing a kiss across the dry cheek. Celia stared curiously at them both.

"I'm fine dear, surprising after that journey. My poor knees." She twisted in her chair. "Clare can you bring Rosie a cuppa?"

"I'll fetch it." Celia offered. She sensed an awkwardness between the women. It wasn't like her mum to be subdued and Clare seemed so shy.

Every year her mum invited the family down to Devon for each birthday and Christmas but Clare politely refused. They had other engagements or mother couldn't face the journey. So Rosie and family would travel up to Nottingham on special occasions but, not being invited to stay, would bunk up at a friend of Rosie's. She always seemed delighted but her own children had to be farmed out, which made Rosie feel they were a family of cuckoos. So the visits to Nottingham became fewer and they took to sending letters, photo's and vouchers in greeting cards. Celia and Ewan barely knew their cousins and it seemed her mum blamed uncle Simon.

The two brothers strolled, side by side into the room, their demeanour relaxed and commanding. Both were tall and burly but the one had the physique of a fitness instructor while the other the paunch of a drinker. Grace's face lit up. She raised herself out of the chair to wave across to her sons, proudly calling their names. Neither looked across to her.

"I hope you've left us some tea." Simon warned. Then, as an after thought, "Hello sis."

Rosie responded with an insincere nod and smile at her brothers as she hurried over to Dan who was just struggling in with an armful of logs. Overlooked, Grace had sunk back into her chair to stare mournfully at the cat. John moved towards the Aga, seemingly to warm his hands. He too ignored his mother but scrutinized Celia. "You've grown. You put me in mind of your mother at this age. But ne' mind, with luck you'll grow out of it." And he laughed heartily. Simon was the only one to join in.

"I don't know if you've noticed but the Aga's gas." He informed Dan. Who exchanged sarcasm for sarcasm. "Yeh. I had noticed. These are for the lounge fire. I didn't think we'd fancy sitting in the kitchen all evening."

"In that case, John and I will take our whiskys and newspapers in there."Simon responded "Forget the tea Clare."

Immediately, Grace heaved herself up and, with cup rattling in its saucer, followed the men through. Clare grabbed a travelling rug off the back of a chair and went after her. From the kitchen, the others listened to Grace complaining and Simon telling her to be quiet if she wanted to stay.

Celia and Ewan hurried to the back door, pausing to ask Niall, who was staring moodily out to the gardens, if he wanted to explore with them. "No thanks." he said and headed for the stairs. Rosie rapped on the window. "Don't go far you two. It's getting dark." The two women started unpacking the food and washing pots. Just as Rosie put her hands into the bubbly water Clare announced, "Guess what? There's a dishwasher behind this cupboard door." Rosie chuckled. "That's a relief. Imagine all the pots with this crowd. Anyway, how are you doing?"

"I'm alright. I'm just a bit worried about Grace. She's getting so frail."

Rosie knew what those worries were. "I bet he doesn't help. He's still bloody heartless I see, up to his old tricks acting king of the castle. He is still up to his old tricks then is he?"Clare didn't respond but her head drooped.

"It can't be easy in that household, looking after mum." Rosie scrutinized the woman's side profile. A sigh, then a quiet, "It's ok." was the response. So Rosie changed the subject. "Despite my brothers, I'm looking forward to this week. There's some fabulous places to visit. Walks by the lakes, old market towns to poke around, getting to know you better and the kids getting to know each other too. It's a shame, after all, they are cousins. Have you got any ideas of what you'd like to do?"

Clare looked alarmed. "Oh, I don't mind. I'll do whatever everyone else wants."

"You're easy to please! I tell you what I don't want to do, at least not tonight." Rosie wiped down the sink. "And that's cook! How do you feel about fish and chips?"

"I doubt Simon will want fish and chips." Clare responded instantly.

"Fuck Simon." Rosie said. "Sorry, but if he wants a three course meal he can cook it himself, He's obviously not changed then?"

Clare studied the inside of the fridge. Thought the best thing to do was change the subject, "How's your job going Rosie? Are you still an Adult Ed teacher?"

"You've got that one wrong. I've never been an Adult Ed teacher." Rosie looked askance.

"Oh? That's what Simon said your job was."

"Hah! Typical. He wouldn't want to broadcast the true nature of my work, that would admit it happens."

"Admit what happens?" Clare looked confused.

"I work for a charity called 'Women's Space'. We support women who are suffering domestic abuse." Rosie noticed Clare's face cloud but carried on, "I facilitate The Freedom Programme which helps women understand what's happened to them and pick their self esteem up off the floor." She changed the subject. "What about you? Are you hoping to go back to nursing. I seem to remember you really loved it."

"No chance. Grace is a full time job." Clare began leafing nervously through a cook book.

"You deserve a medal, she'd drive me nuts."

With that and to Clare's relief, Rosie then suggested they should check out the bedrooms and arm in arm they strolled upstairs.

Later, hunger drove everyone back into the lounge where the brothers were both asleep and snoring, heads lolling against the back of the settee, mouths wide open and papers jumbled on their knees. Across the room, Grace was also asleep, legs folded neatly to one side and glasses perched on the end of her nose. They flinched in alarm and bustled with their papers when Celia and Ewan bounced in, noisily followed by the others. Only Bethany was missing.

"I'm starving." stated Celia.

"Good."said Rosie. "I thought we could have fish and chips tonight."

"Good idea." Dan agreed. "No washing up."

"Yes. Chips. Yes." Celia shouted.

"I love fish and chips." Ewan said.

"I hope the chip shop's not far, I'm hungry." John added.

"Well, I don't want fish and chips." stated Simon.

Clare stared silently down at her hands.

"OK. John, you can fetch them. It's not many minutes into Keswick by car. Simon, there's plenty of stuff in the fridge you can cook yourself something with." Rosie instructed in a no nonsense voice. Both men spluttered but before either could object Bethany flounced in. "There's nothing to do in this place." She threw some magazines down on the table. "I haven't even got a tele in my room."

"I hate to break it to you but there's only two T.V's and your dad's got one of them." Dan tried not to gloat.

"What am I going to do for a whole week?" Bethany turned to her mum, she looked distraught. "And what's for dinner?"

"We're just sorting that darling."

Rosie had grabbed a pad and was taking the orders. Simon knew he was outvoted, all he could do was insist on plaice NOT cod or haddock."

John meekly took the pad and left.

Round the table, candles lit, bottles of wine opened and fish and chips on their plates, the families began to unwind.Grace recited seaside holidays with her two naughty boys but when Celia asked her to tell them about mum, she merely called Rosie 'A rebellious girl who was always arguing with her. At which, Rosie began to argue, John said 'See what she means?' Simon laughed and Celia looked across in solidarity with her mum. Bethany spent most of the dinnertime complaining about a smear of tomato sauce on her new crop top. Ewan, who had ordered two whole fish and was beginning to feel a little bilious, was surreptitiously trying to pass pieces of fish under the table to the dog.

"Don't feed that dog at the table, young man."Simon instructed.

"His name's Ewan." Dan retorted, staring pointedly at the cat curled up on Grace's knee.

Bethany got up and left the room, ignoring her mother's instruction to take her plate away and Clare's hands started fiddling with the table cloth.

"Is there anything for pudding?" Grace looked at Clare but Rosie spoke up.

"There's always that box of chocolates you've got hidden behind you mum."

Reluctantly, Grace fishd out the chocolates from behind the cushion and handed them round.

"I saw a box of Jenga bricks in the cupboard." Celia said. "Should we have a go?"

"I'm afraid my hands aren't steady enough." Grace said.

"We're nipping to the pub." John headed for his coat in the hallway, Simon close behind and again, Grace's face fell.

Niall had no idea what Jenga was. Puzzles or board games were unheard of in their family. He refused to play but watched as the Morris family teased each other throughout the steady dismantling of bricks. He had to admit it, it looked good fun.

Saturday

The Clash of Characters

Clare sat at the kitchen table. She never slept well the first night in a strange bed, it felt as if she was subconsciously on some kind of guard duty, listening out for invaders. She had this constant niggle that she was born into the wrong century and should be living in feudal times, riding round on horseback, taking produce to the villagers or tending her strip of land and defending the corner of the country from marauders. Also, early morning felt like her time. A time to watch the sky turn black shapes in the tiny patch of grass and bushes at home become distinguishable and the orange sliver of sun to appear over the horizon. This helped calm her despairing thoughts, gather resolve and prepare her for whatever the day (Simon) may bring. This homely old kitchen, its pale pine cupboards housing modern appliances, hiding their ugliness and noise away, the maroon Aga giving off its constant, comforting heat, the cat stretched out luxuriously at its base, the plate lined Welsh dresser and thick old walls painted in a midnight purple all suggested a gentler bygone era and calmed her troubled mind. A week of company and change, if she could just overcome her anxiety.

As was her habit, Clare leaned 'The Times' against the teapot with a determined flourish. She would learn about current affairs, she would understand politics, what was happening in Parliament, in Britain, in the world. But somehow, after she had read the captions under the pictures on the front page, she found her mind wandered. It was as if politics, the news, the world was too cruel and seedy to be real life. When she believed the news it scared her. The way she thought humans should behave was so far removed from those daily headlines calmly reporting Wars and financial fraud as if they were rational and reasonable exchanges made her feel disconnected from the whole of humanity, let alone a newspaper leaning on a teapot. She chewed at her nails and resolved to read the article announcing the death of George Harrison but found it too sad.

Dawn was just a crack of cream light on the horizon when a face appeared at the kitchen window, causing her to leap up from the table with a yell, spilling her coffee across the open newspaper. The figure started waving madly and was calling out.

"Auntie Clare, it's me. It's Sapphire."

"Sapphire?"

"Can you let me in? It's freezing out here."

The body slid away from the window and the face became hazily distorted through the round stained glass on the door.

Clare peered through the glass. "Oh my God. What are you doing here this time of the morning?" She cautiously opened the door and like a spring tide, the young woman tumbled in.

Clare caught a whiff of the dawn air, a promise of nature's clean bouquet, so different to the metallic fumes of the city It awakened an ancient yearning, a promise just for a moment but then was gone, locked outside again as the door slid shut.

"Thank you. It's a good job you were up." Sapphire started to strip off her pink jacket and unwind a purple scarf. "I managed to get a lift almost all the way here luckily. Have you ever walked across furrowed fields in the dark? Auntie, how are you? I haven't seen you in ages." The girl's eyes were full of fun, her slim body a force of energy as she hugged Clare, bringing a sense of love and joy for life.

"I barely recognized you Sapphire" Clare mumbled into her shoulder "You're a young woman. Surely you've not travelled up from Uni at this time of the morning?"

"No, no. Didn't mum tell you? I've been to Stonehenge"

"To visit the stones?"

She laughed. "Well yes, but it was the Goddess festival Aunt Clare. It was amazing."

"And you've travelled all the way up here on your own? What trains are going at this time?"

"I hitch hiked. That's why I was so lucky, I got a local. Boy, this place is gorgeous."

Sapphire stretched her arms to indicate the whole cottage and surrounds.

Clare's eyes widened as thoughts crowded. Simon would say 'Height of foolishness. Fancy her parents letting her wander around the country on her own, accepting lifts from strangers' but she just smiled. "It's so lovely to see you after all this time."

"I'm going to go and wake the parents up now" Sapphire giggled, heading for the stairs.

Clare listened to the little delighted screams, bumps and laughter going on upstairs for a moment and troubled thoughts popped into her mind. 'Why wasn't her family like that? Why did they always bicker or worse, ignore each other? Why did she feel so miserable, like she didn't belong with them?' she shook her head. 'No, they were just different, more reserved, they would be there if this gloom ever got the better of me, wouldn't they?' and she hurried to make coffee for her family.

The sun was peering through each window now, like a promise. The house began to stir. Toilets flushed, voices travelled the upstairs co-rridor.

"Have you got my Tee shirt again Bethany?" Niall accused across the landing.

"Piss off. As if I'd wear your stuff." was the angry retort.

"Bethany, there's no need..." Clare's voice called up, then slurred off, as if being silenced.

"What's that dog doing up here?" Simon, irritated.

"Think it's been in their bedroom all night dad." Niall's voice boastful, the informer.

"If we lose our deposit Rosie, it'll be your problem."

"She's been on her own blanket all night"

"If she has an accident up here...."

"She won't. She's well trained."

"Their was that hotel in Wales." Dan's voice, full of mischief.

"Shut up Dan" Rosie giggled "You've managed to wake everybody up Sapphy."

"Sorry guys" she bounced back down the stairs "Tell you what, I'll make breakfast for everyone."

"Good. And tell Clare to bring me a cup of tea up" Simon called down.

Niall and Bethany added their ha'porth to the instructions.

"Full English for me"

"Poached eggs on toast for me"

Sapphire and Clare exchanged glances on the stairs as they squeezed past, teacup rattling in Clare's hand.

Celia stuck a dishevelled head out of the room she was sharing with her brother and shrieked. Her sister hurried back up the stairs two at a time.

"Is that Sapphy I can hear?" Celia ran across the corridor and threw herself at her sister, wrapping long limbs around her. Sapphire grabbed the wooden pineapple topping the balustrade to steady herself and prevent being toppled back down to the turn on the stair. "Steady on sis." But she was laughing heartily as they hugged. Ewan was sneaking up behind, gathering up Celia's dressing gown cords to tie the girls together, his boyish way of showing affection.

Meanwhile Dan was responding to the food orders. "What did your lot's last servant die of?" he called out.

'Good old Dan' thought Rosie.

"Well, she did offer" responded Bethany, already talking on her phone, reminding her friend Jules that they must keep up the phone censure of a disrespectful girl at school. Her friend responded 'She's already turned Mel and Sheena against you.' Bethany's lips were tight, thin lines, 'Bitch. I'll sort her when I get back.' With a satisfied laugh, she threw her phone on the bed and pouting, checked her dark, long curls in the mirror then the pink array of clothes hung carefully in the wardrobe.

"What's all this racket about you lot?" John's disgruntled voice travelled through his bedroom door. "What time do you call this?"

Niall and Ewan were taking stock of each other. Ewan, tall and skinny and Niall, smaller but heavier with shoulders that would be the envy of many a rugby player, yellow hair in straight short wires, like his father and the stare of someone used to getting his own way.

"Couldn't you manage to get your p.j's to match up?" Niall stared at Ewan's blue Star Wars bottoms and orange Spider Man top.

"Guess I'm not that bothered" Ewan shrugged "Heh. Do you want to go exploring all those outhouses today?"

"No thanks. I've got Star Wars to explore."

A strong smell of cigars and a cloud drifted towards the group on the landing, the shadowy figure of Uncle John behind. He coughed. "How good a full English can a teenager make? Why don't we let Clare cook breakfast?"

Simon agreed. "Or Rosie."

Dan burst out of the bedroom. "Or one of you two even?"

Simon poked his head round his bedroom door "Don't be ridiculous."

"No point in having a dog and barking yourself" added John.

Dan called back into his room "Rosie this is going to be SUCH fun. A holiday with not one but two chauvinists! They're going to let you cook breakfast. Isn't that nice for you?"

By the way the two men ignored his comment Dan wondered if they even knew what the word chauvinist meant, let alone the possibility of being one.

Later, as the two families were sat round the pine kitchen table with Sapphire and Clare rushing from oven to table, trying to slither eggs onto plates and pour tea or coffee over shoulders without scalding anyone, Simon decided this was a good time to explore the subject of

Sapphire's seemingly unlimited freedom.

"So what time did you get here Sapphire?"

"Oh I guess it was sevenish."

"And you say you hitchhiked?"

"Yes I did Uncle Simon."

"And did you two know about this?" Simon looked at Rosie and Dan with disdain.

Rosie smiled towards Sapphy "She knows how to look after herself." "I'd have thought it's not her you'd worry about but other people," Simon reached for the full English Clare was offering.

Dan paused from the task of pulling a lump of chewing gum out of Ewan's hair."Oh our Saph' wouldn't hurt a soul."

Simon grimaced. "You know what I mean."

"You mean men."

Simon chose to ignore this comment. "Aren't you worried about her safety? It seems so irresponsible to condone her behaviour"

With his dad distracted Ewan took the opportunity to pull away from the rather painful procedure being inflicted on his head.

"But as you said it's not her behaviour we're concerned about is it?"

"But she's asking for trouble."

"So, what you're saying Simon, is that Sapphire should restrict her own life, her own freedom because there are guys out there who can't control themselves?" A sliver of chewing gum flew across and landed on the butter dish as Dan gestured towards his daughter.

Bethany glanced up sharply from her phone, this conversation was getting interesting. Hippy Dan was putting her dad right. This was a first! He'd never win though, no-one ever did. She'd never heard her dad talk about sex before, it was a bit of a taboo subject in their household. even though she was one of those girls who dressed to attract the male gaze. She liked it, it was her power and her dad never objected. Bethany knew there was an unspoken element of danger in this. She always told her friends that men couldn't help themselves, couldn't control their sexual urges when a beautiful girl came on to them. And this uncle of hers was saying of course they could control themselves, taking away her power. Well, maybe sometime this week she'd come on to HIM. Then he'd change his tune. He was pretty cute in a docile, unaware of it way. The thought of seducing her uncle, his helplessness before her sexual onslaught, made Bethany's insides turn to slush and she glanced round the room as if to check that no-one had noticed.

The two mens' voices were starting to raise. Clare anxiously started tidying the magazines on the coffee table, trying to appear casual, though listening, ready to distract them if need be.

"Well,you can't entirely blame them, can you? Here's an attractive young woman, in shorts no less, trying to get in their car with them."

Dan shook his head, "So you think that's an invitation for sex, do you?"

Three young heads shot up, for a moment abandoning their breakfasts.

Grace looked alarmed "You two, there are young children present."

Simon turned back to Sapphy "Don't you think it's the height of foolishness young lady, to be hitching round the country in the middle of the night?"He looked smug.

A cloud passed over her face but she smiled at her uncle.

"Well, I started hitching right outside the festival, everybody does, it's nearly all young people. It's like a parallel universe all about peace, love and community."

Sapphy closed her eyes and like a virtual reality image her mind's eye took her back to the Goddess Festival. There was the swaying crowd singing to the distant figures of the Medieval Maidens on the greenery entwined stage, darkness cloaking the red remnants of sunset lighting up the ancient pillars of Stonehenge. She could smell the wafts of pizzas, burgers and chips and her insides flipped as she pictured the copse of trees and the musician she kissed goodbye to before leaving the sacred site.

"I don't know why a young woman like you, from a respectable family, would want to mix with hooligans at one of those rowdy festivals." Simon's accusation brought her out of her reverie.

Sapphy glanced at her mum, paused. "Uncle Simon, the Goddess Festival is about nature and peace. There are no fights and all the profits go to environmental causes. What can possibly be criminal about that?"

"Young women should not be exposed to these things."

"Young women run this festival Uncle Simon. It's Pagan, based on the Goddess and nature, a far cry from the patriarchy, Wars and commerce our world otherwise endures.

Simon spluttered but before he could reply Dan spoke up.

"I think we'd better leave it at that. Come and sit down and finish your breakfast Sapphire." But he winked as she angrily plonked down beside him.

"Clare, come on and join us." Rosie called "Your breakfast is getting cold."

But Simon was still on his soap box. "I've seen some of those festival crowds on T.V. I wouldn't trust any one of them. I certainly wouldn't let my kids anywhere near the place."

Niall spoke up "I wouldn't want to go, dad. They all look so scruffy."

Clare sat down at the table, "They certainly seem to put on some top musicians." She handed a pair of scissors to Dan. "You might find it easier with these."

Dan hauled his son and plonked the squirming lad in front of him again.

Simon scowled at his wife. "Trust you. You'll be wanting to go next."

"Simon, you may choose the Rotary club and Young Farmers balls, if you'll pardon the expression, for your social life but we happen to prefer more 'down to earth' events." Rosie slammed the teapot down on the table.

Unnoticed, the dog was visiting every person at the table, working her way round, checking each lap for spillages, staring appealingly at each face, her brown eyes getting bigger and bigger. When Simon, then Bethany pushed her away she looked offended and crept back to Celia who slipped a whole slice of bacon and toast under the tablecloth.

Uncle John, who had been calmly eating, now took an expansive drag on his cigar and leaned back in his seat, "I've seen some of them bands on T.V. Bloody row if you ask me. I don't know why they'd pay a fortune to listen to 'em. Tents packed in like sardines, drugs going on everywhere, scruffy, lawless louts. Peace and love my arse, No thank you, Stonehenge hell I'd call it."

"Exactly." Simon agreed.

"And I'd say that Cloud cottage is the right name for this place." Rosie coughed and flapped cigar smoke away from her muesli. " So, what are the plans for the day?"

There was a silence. Simon glanced at his phone, " I've got a business meeting on the golf course at 11."

Rosie's face dropped, "I thought we'd all be doing something together today, our first day."

Bethany had finished her eggs, "I've got better things to do than sit around with you lot." She got up, already back on her phone, and headed for the stairs.

"Nip and fetch me brown coat will you Rosie" Grace instructed, still eating, "It's very draughty in here."

For someone who swore she could only eat small amounts of food little and often, she had already devoured two bowls of porridge and was tucking into sausage, eggs and toast.

John got up. "Mother, you need to start taking iron tablets. If anyone needs me today, I'll be in the first real ale pub you get to in Keswick."

"So, you're leaving Clare to look after the kids then Simon, are you?" Clare shot Rosie a look, half gratitude, half warning "As well as just getting up from the table."

Simon didn't appear bothered, "I thought we were all here to enjoy ourselves, sis."

"ALL being the operative word!" Rosie said, banging plates together as she picked them up. "I'll clear this lot up." Dan spoke up. "What are you and Clare going to do?"

Simon threw him a look that spoke of letting the side down.

"I've heard it's a lovely walk into Keswick" said Clare "I thought I mi-ght do that if the kids wanted to. Oh but what about..." and she flicked her head towards Grace, who was cramming eggs into her mouth, quite unaware.

"She'll be alright. Has she got her knitting?" Rosie replied. " I'd like to come with you, if you don't mind?"

"I think I'd better stay with her." Clare looked crestfallen.

"I'll come as long as there's a games store." Niall said without enthusiasm.

"I'm happy to keep Niall company," Ewan smiled at his cousin, who scowled in response, "If you must."

Rosie looked questioningly at Celia.

"I think I'll stay here. I'm going to find a hidden corner so I can read my new fantasy book in peace." Celia held up a hardback book. The cover showed a teenage girl astride a huge black horse, mane flowing as it reared up onto its back legs, a full moon as background.

"Looks good." Rosie smiled.

"I can't wait." Celia called as she waved and ran out of the room.

"I'll stay here as well and keep my eye on gran. I want to do a bit of practicing anyway and catch up on the Z's, if dad's alright and you don't need me with you mum?" Sapphire picked up her guitar and started strumming.

Simon tutted, "She plays guitar as well. I'm so glad I'm going out." He took his camel coat off the peg. Rosie mouthed to Dan 'Only Fools and horses'.

"Me too" John agreed, "we don't need that row all week."

"I bet you wouldn't say that if it was Niall." Dan slammed open the dishwasher door.

"Girls are not known for being rock guitarists." Simon said calmly.

Seeing her dad's face, Sapphire hurried over and hugged him, nearly knocking Dan into the dishwasher, then still strumming, she headed outside and perched on the wall, "It's lovely and sunny out here."

"That's it. Push your dad into the dishwasher then let's get it started." Rosie said and Ewan giggled as he imagined his dad, cramped inside, sprayed with bubbly water and then blow dried.

At last, the cat and dog seemed to have come to some kind of arrangement. The cat had claimed the higher ground, he haughtily strolled over to the kitchen units and in one fluid motion, leapt up to check his bowl for tidbits. While below, the dog padded behind Dan getting in his way and staring up beseechingly.

"There we are then, thank you Sapphy, if you're sure, everybody's sorted." Clare said in relief.

The group grabbed coats and stepped out to a choir of blackbirds and the backing tenors of droning bees among the hydrangeas, all busily filling up, fattening their bodies in readiness for the deprivations of winter. Clare leaned on the wall and breathed in deeply the clear air. That sharp promise of winter. "I do so love the countryside, what a treat this is." She studied the ruby and gold trees swaying from sunlit hills, the crystal clatter of the brook rushing over brown carp and stones towards the S bend of the river below. And beyond, in oranges and browns, the Skiddaw mountain range convening with clouds and hawks.

"Couldn't you move out of Nottingham then?" Rosie spoke from behind her.

"Oh no, Simon would never live somewhere like this. He can't stand it."

"It's not just about Simon though, is it? Rosie put her hand on the other woman's shoulder. "I don't know how you cope with him, he's such a selfish bugger, always has been. When we were kids he was a right bully, mum and dad spoiled him rotten, he always got his own way and they always believed him. I think they were scared of his tantrums, so they placated him, creating a monster. It was no fun, I can tell you. And I bet it's no fun for you now, is it?"

The familiar panic rose up like bile through Clare's stomach, her face flushed and hands picked at moss between the stones. But she replied calmly, not to give anything away. "I've got a good life really. The kids keep me busy, I have a nice house , look after Grace, it's fulfilling."

"That's good then." Rosie called, not very convincingly, as she disappeared into the gloom of a yew hedge and clicked open a wrought iron gate onto open moorland.

Clare ran to catch up through the rusty old gate, looked up and took a sharp breath. Glowing purple heather stretched over the moor towards the hills. A full orange sun was forcing its face through gold tinted clouds. She stopped abruptly, and misery, that old spectre, ambushed by a landscape in watercolours, fled.

"It's so beautiful." but the words escaped into the wind. A jumble of emotions arose, crammed into her mind where the dull misery had just crouched. Hope resided in these halls of vast sky. Change sang down the great sails of wind. Peace sprang up from the purple scented heather. The promise of a new life beamed from the sunlit heavens. Clare sobbed, joy and sadness overwhelmed her and she threw up her arms.

She saw the boys charging full pelt down the hill, she saw Niall was laughing, she saw pheasants clattering clumsily up into the sky ahead of them and she saw Rosie pointing. She was saying something.

"Look at that bird of prey" And she saw the huge bird, wings bronzed and glinting, outstretched almost motionless, gliding the currents of air.Its high pitched shriek was a call to arms, a summons to freedom.

The boys tried to mimic it but then stopped as another hawk replied from the top branch of a Scots pine. The women watched as the white Audi purred by on the narrow lane, elegant against the muddy tractors and battered jeeps parked in gateways, Simon at the wheel, a muted Fleetwood Mac through the window.

"Off to his golf." Rosie scoffed.

The majestic clouds moving across the big sky and over the fields made Clare feel quite wild and free. She so wanted to, yet was unable to confide in this woman who understood but whose brother, and her jailer, was somewhere in the town that was now appearing in the golden light of the valley below. It felt as if he would hear her and whisper into her head 'How could you tell my sister such lies? Why are you betraying me like this?' She rubbed the back of her hand across her eyes as tears brimmed. Rosie had noticed but said no more.

Niall hated to admit it but he was really enjoying himself. Out in the real world, running wild behind Ewan. For his cousin could name birds, spot nests and rabbit burrows and smell foxes. The most vicious fights on his screen had not helped Niall escape to such freedom. The hill was now behind them, an alluring gap into the chill gloom of the trees ahead and he wanted to run and run and carry on running. He passed Ewan, his mother was now a blob of colour beside a rock, his father a larger white blob cruising away. The relief was intense. The aching, angry rock he carried round in his heart had shifted leaving a sense of being fiercely alive. He was aware of the earth under the grass bustling with life, creatures digging, burrowing. He felt the playful gusts of the wind, spirits singing into his ear, pine scent urging him to the trees. High, high up the clouds moving fast in white battalions. This was life. This was freedom. This was nature calling 'Join us'. And Niall laughed.

"Wait for me" Ewan called, and he stopped, lungs filling and heart pumping.

No sooner had everyone left than Grace felt alone. Their selfishness annoyed her. 'Where was that girl? She needed a cup of tea. She shouldn't have to get up and go looking for help at her age.' Rosie had put a small hand bell on the table and reaching out, Grace shook it firmly.

With a smile, Sapphire put down her guitar, she knew she would not get to practice or have a snooze now. So they took their teas into the sunny, plant filled conservatory and Grace started to talk, well, it was more complaining - about the cleaning woman back home who, it seemed, moved everything round in Grace's rooms just to annoy her yet never got round to vacuuming under the settee. Then, about her daughter in law, who sometimes brought her dinner late and not as hot as it could be and nearly always forgot something off the shopping list. Neither did she stay with her all day, as Simon had instructed but left at four to be in their part of the house for when the kids came home from school. At least that was her excuse. Surely at their age the kids could look after themselves for an hour or two? Clare wouldn't still be holding a grudge after the time she accused her of stealing her jewellery box, now would she? The cleaning woman again, putting her things in the bottom of the wardrobe. She had apologized to Clare after all and that was not easy.

"And I'm not well, you know. People forget I'm 85. Just because I keep my wits about me and make an effort" she patted her powdered brown face and pouted her thin red lips. "I used to be a very attractive woman, all the men were after me. I don't think your grandfather appreciated how much of a catch I was."

Sapphire winced. "Did you work grandma?"

"Oh yes. I taught piano right up to when I had John."

Couldn't you get childcare?"

"It wasn't that dear. Women had to leave work after having a baby in those days."

"Unbelievable"

"It was quite alright. Men were the breadwinners.Those of us who worked only went out to buy the extras."

"So you're saying you didn't miss your work, your colleagues, your own money and independence?"

Grace's eyes pained for a second, then brusquely " That was the way it was. We all just got on with it."

"So you were quite a pianist then?"

"Yes, some said I could have been on stage as a classical pianist."

"And if you had been a man you probably would have. Does that not make you angry Gran?"

"It's no good dwelling on what could have been, is it? I had a family to look after and a husband who provided a roof over our heads." Suddenly, Sapphire sensed the years of boredom, of frustration and lack of fulfillment and appreciation this old woman had endured. Stuck in the house like so many women of the time, talents and brains reduced to child talk and housework. And how afraid they were of rocking the boat, of challenging. The generation of stiff upper lip women. Women who were briefly allowed to take over the men's jobs, earn a wage and experience freedom during the War but were hastily bundled back into the homes in the 1950's. The decade of women's neuroses.

The young woman experienced a rush of gratitude towards her free thinking parents and the steady progress of equality activated by their rebellious generation. She put tea and cake beside her gran's chair and covered her knees with a travelling rug, knowing not to look at the old woman when asking questions so it would be easier for her to answer.

"Tell me about yourself when you were growing up. I'd like to hear about your life."

Grace realized that here, in this grandchild she barely knew, was someone she could confide in, who would not dismiss her long buried distress. For a few minutes she was that happy girl, then the young woman, full of dreams, bursting with life and the thrill of nurturing a huge musical talent. So she talked about her piano exams and the encouragement from her teachers as entranced, they listened to her playing. But, with the nothing to lose attitude of the old, Grace, now furious, asked the young woman why no one had warned her, had not given her any instruction on the joyous danger of sex? Sapphire knew not to look alarmed and smiled her encouragement. Grace continued, back in the past. 'I thought I loved Edward, he said he loved me and the passion was so powerful. I know now it was lust, as he knew all along. And then Edward was gone, moved down south and I was left, alone and pregnant, to face my parents."

Sapphire glanced at the stricken face. She sensed the misery the younger Grace must have endured. It was still there, the anger flashing in those old eyes, tears in the wrinkles.

"My parents made me go away to have the baby.They put him up for adoption. It was only the intervention of my mother's sister that persuaded them to let me keep John. They were so ashamed you see, you have no idea what it was like then. Their friends disowned them, I had to come out of music college and Edward had merely moved to another university, completely denying any involvement." Sapphire watched as the emotions moved across her nan's face as her dreams crashed and the anger turned inwards. Everyone had blamed her but Grace had a strong sense of injustice.

There was a silence as the woman became lost in thought. The only sound was the rhythmic tick of the old grandfather clock in the lounge, Sapphire sat cross legged on the rug by her slippered feet, not moving but waiting. The room seemed to lean in, as if listening and waiting too. The young woman sensed a chill and pulled the blanket up around her gran's neck. Grace continued.

"The world was too strong for me though. I had to accept my punishment. I have felt so aggrieved Sapphire. My talents were as great as Edwards but he was able to continue his studies and just move on with his life. It never affected him and I never saw him again. I was left to bring up John as best I could. Of course, at that time it was women's work so my mother and aunt helped. I can see now, John was given mixed messages from early on. He was a beautiful child, with golden curls and blue eyes, the 'Pears soap boy' he was called, so the women all spoiled him. But, if relatives came to call John and I were banished to an attic room. And then the men of the family were very strict with him. I think they believed that if they showed John any affection it would somehow indicate to me and my boy we were forgiven. Then I met Harry and he promised to take on John as his own." her voice lowered "But he used to hit him with a belt, while his own son looked on. Your mother was the only one who intervened and she was just a child herself. They were all so harsh, no wonder John has turned out the way he has."

Then Grace abruptly stopped. It was as if the voice inside her head suddenly realized it had said too much and there might well be a price to pay. She looked Sapphire sternly in the eye, "You won't say anything...?" she faltered.

"Of course not gran." Sapphire laid her hand on the old woman's arm. She was trembling, her face was crumpled and the tears of bitterness spilled into her tea but reassured, she continued with her story.

"I have never lived my life looking forward to what could be but backwards at the regret and shame. And look at what the boy I sacrificed everything for turned into," she whispered. "He is intolerable, but how can I blame him? I tried to enjoy being a mother but I was so unhappy a lot of the time. I'm afraid I often took it out on your mother, the only one who seemed to care."

Sapphire wiped away her own tears. "And how can you blame yourself Gran? It was the society you grew up in that was cruel, not you. It was a mistake, that's all. It's happened to some of my friends and everyone rushed to help. Their parents have helped with the child, the guys have taken responsibility too and their parents have helped. Then the women have been able to carry on at university. It's not ideal but they manage and the child is loved. So you see, times have changed. Edward and his family should have taken some responsibility , you should have been given encouragement without that bloody awful guilt and then John could have been brought up with love, dignity and discipline, as all children should be. All the friends who turned their backs, the men with their Victorian values and the women who didn't have the nerve to challenge their hypocrisy, they should be the ones ashamed, not you." Again, needing reassurance. "You won't say anything will you?" Grace took Sapphire's hand and gripped it tightly "Thank you dear." The two women leaned their heads back against the cushions and were quiet.

Dan wended his way up to the little sitting room at the top of the house. An old oak desk fronted vivid blue peacocks amongst birch trees, wallpaper that looked as if it was from the Edwardian era. He couldn't wait to show Rosie. But the sunlit mountain view through the skylight was even more striking. He anticipated browsing the shelves of books, his tea and biscuits and the silence. Yet as soon as he settled into the armchair, worrying thoughts of Rosie clamoured into his mind. 'He knew her brothers of old, how would she cope with their bullying for seven days? She was such a gentle, trusting soul, almost childlike, this was what made her so endearing. As well as her sense of humour of course. How could she possibly have been brought up by the same parents as her siblings? A father who ruled the house with Victorian zeal and a timid mother, unable to protect her children from his discipline and so sided with him. Like Goebbels to Hitler, she meted out his demands, turning the boys into haughty and ambitious tyrants.'

Dan leafed through Ian Mcewan's 'Amsterdam', realizing not a word had sunk in. 'How were they going to deal with the next week of torment? Rosie could be gobby and now it looked like she was taking Clare under her wing, standing up for her. Tonight he would be vigilant.' With this thought, Dan relaxed and the words on the page started to form into a story.

Bethany was in her room, staring into the mirror. 'No point in putting makeup on in this God forsaken place.' she thumbed half heartedly through a catalogue of tattoos, the latest fashion essentials. 'Perhaps the grinning Cheshire cat? Or Kali the Goddess of destruction?' She had to get the money for them out of her dad somehow. He would never agree to pay for tattoos. And she'd have to keep them hidden from him, he'd go berserk if he saw them. One on each bum cheek perhaps, then she'd have a good excuse for sending a sexy picture of her arse to Ramone Brown. And, of course, Charlotte Leavesley, she'd be so jealous. There'd be no way she could afford a tattoo.' Bethany snorted to herself as she rang her closest ally.

"How's things? Is Leavesley trying to squirm her way in with my friends?"

Jules sniggered down the line. "She's offered to take Michelle, Iris and Millie for cocktails in V bar." Bethany sneered, "Hah. They'll never get in. They look their age."

"She knows a barman apparently," her confidante replied.

This annoyed Bethany enough to pull a frowning face at herself in the mirror.

"This fucking place. We're in the middle of nowhere. I wish I'd never come. But you know what my dad's like. That Leavesley's going to get it when I get back. Keep your eye on her for me."

Before her co-conspirator could reply, Bethany threw her phone on the bed and started a hunt for her hidden bottle of vodka.

Once in the town Rosie insisted she was parched and needed a coffee. She hoped that once the lads had gone off to find the games shop Clare might open up and confide, she was obviously miserable and desperate to talk to someone. Clare half heartedly studied the covers of novels in the old bookshop while Rosie secured a table in a secluded corner and ordered coffees.

"They've got fabulous cakes in here." she ventured as Clare plonked herself down onto the wicker seat opposite. "The tiffin is known as death by chocolate."

"Oh no, I'd better not." Clare signalled towards her stomach. "But you get some if you want."

"I know that old ruse. I'm going to get you some or I'll finish up sharing mine!"

"No, no. I wouldn't do that." Clare looked distressed.

"I was only joking. I'm sorry. Dan does it all the time." Rosie grabbed her hand across the table. "Are you alright sweetie? I didn't mean to upset you."

"I'm o.k. It's just I did that to Simon once and he wasn't impressed."

"Yes well, he's an idiot isn't he!" Rosie studied the gentle face opposite trying to control the wobbling lip and brimming eyes. "You know you can talk to me anytime. I may be his sister but I do know what that man is like."

"I think I'd better check where Niall's gone."

Like a tortured spirit Clare abruptly got up to cross the road to the boys, hardly noticing the cars slowing down or the angry glares of the drivers as she stepped out. The drinks arrived. Rosie hastily slurped down the hot latte and shoved the biscuits in her pocket to chase Clare across to the games shop. She was stood forlornly in the corner of the fantasy section, surrounded by pictures of heroes, dragons and evil cloaked rulers. 'An appropriate place.' Rosie mused wryly. Then spotted the boys, who had obviously not seen them, giggling at the picture of a semi naked heroine on the cover of a game. Squashed together amongst dusty shelves this heroine hugged her sobbing sister in law while the shopkeeper watched suspiciously from the front counter.

When Niall finally saw them he looked anxiously towards his mum, so Rosie guided her to the lads. "Grab the game you want Niall. We're leaving."

Clare was trying to compose herself but couldn't speak. Rosie paid the staring shopkeeper, glared at Ewan who started to complain about having to leave and 'what was up anyway?' and ushered them all out of the shop. The doorbell clanged behind them like an accusation.

"I think we'd better go back to the cottage." Rosie said. "We can come and explore Keswick later."

Alarmed, Niall walked beside his mum, scrutinizing her face as she stumbled, unseeing, past shop windows exhibiting exotic packages of soaps and creams, their herbal scents drifting out towards them. Handmade leather bags and satchels swung gently in doorways. 'Come in. Come in' they beckoned. Mounds, truckles and pyramids of assorted cheeses wafted their milky scent out to the street. A leafy paper bower framed stacks of books, enticing titles and cover illustrations called soundlessly 'Come in and read me.'

Rosie hesitated at each tempting doorway, glanced at her companion, sighed and engaged stiff upper lip with the thought 'Another time.'

"She'll be alright." Rosie told Niall. "Don't you worry now."

And Ewan put his arm around the boy's shoulder. This time Niall didn't push it off.

They hustled past the busy shops and congested pavements to the river path where the houses thinned out.

A sombre bell rang out across the valley, a wild lane leading to a wooden gate into the church yard. In the eaves of the steeple bats swooped, claiming their territory in readiness for their upside down hibernation, undeterred by the lights of candles and sounds of zealous singing below. A breeze scuttled over grass and dead blooms in jars, the residents below their stones, oblivious to the group passing quietly by.

"Do you see the rook's nest right up at the top of those trees?" Ewan pointed up into the high and wide canopies of a row of Elm trees. The birds loud cawing was like the gossiping din of deaf old men, all talking at once. There would be a flash of black wing amongst the vibrant green and browns of the seasonal leaves. But now Niall barely glanced up. His mouth was drawn down and forehead lined as he watched Clare.

"What's up with mum?"

"I don't know but I bet mum will help her."

"She goes like this sometimes." Niall said. "I think dad does this to her. Or do you think it's me?"

"It's not you. Your dad's not very nice to her, is he!" Ewan ventured.

"No, he's not." And Niall rushed back to the forlorn figure to slip his hand into hers.

After the initial surprise at this display of affection Clare smiled gratefully at her son and was cheered.

Beyond the gate, alongside the walkers the wheat was now short, sharp rows of straws stretching yellow across the field. Soon the fields would burn and the villagers would be rushing to get their washing in before smoke drifted across their gardens.

Once back at the cottage, Clare hurried upstairs to her room to think and Rosie turned into the kitchen. And, there were the three young rebels, muddy hands shuffling through packages in the fridge.

"There's only cheese and olives" complained Celia "I hate olives."

"And sour old yoghourt" agreed Ewan in disgust "Yuk. Where's the sweet stuff?"

"Should we make cupcakes? I've got chocolate." said Rosie from the doorway.

"Ooh yes." Celia's head bashed on the fridge shelf and she stepped on Niall's feet as she hastily backed out of the fridge.

"Ouch." Niall fell back against Ewan who shoved him in response.

"Go and wash your mucky hands, you lot and I'll get the ingredients ready." Rosie laughed.

"I don't need to wash my hands. I've only been reading a book." Celia exclaimed, then on seeing Rosie's expression, started to follow the boys out of the kitchen, pausing in the doorway.

"We don't have to wait till dinner to eat 'em, do we?" she asked, "This isn't your way of getting us to make the puddings, is it mum?"

"You cheeky thing. Hurry up before I change my mind."

Rosie flicked on the kettle, made tea and took mugs round to her mother and Sapphire. It all seemed very sombre in the conservatory, the two women stopped their conversation and waited for her to leave the room. She knocked and took tea in to Clare who was sitting thoughtfully on her bed, then huffed her way up the narrow stairs to the next floor, where Dan, absorbed in his book, silently waved his thanks for the tea.

"Charming" Rosie muttered even as she took note of the darkening sky and deep red sunset framed in the narrow window, the soft yellow glow of the lamp illuminating her husband's face poking above a wool blanket. Her face softened. How lovely he was. She crept back and leaned round his chair to kiss the warm lips, her hair a sudden curtain round his face. "Can't stop." she whispered as he curved round in response. "Got to make cakes." And she fled.

"I'll deal with him later." she breathlessly promised herself as she hurried back into the kitchen where her three assistant chefs were waiting, holding up clean hands for inspection. "Would you lot like some homemade elderflower cordial?" she asked.

"Is it alcoholic?" asked Niall, grinning.

"No. Celia, can you get it out of the fridge?"

Celia passed the bottle over to her mum with a wink to the lads. Rosie wondered why they were all surreptitiously watching her as she bustled about getting cake ingredients and making more tea. Until she released the top off the bottle and the drink came bubbling out in an explosion of fizz. All around the room it flew, speckling their faces and dripping down the kitchen units.

"Result." Celia screamed in delight, the lads bent double with mirth.

"Get out." Rosie yelled, her face and hair covered in sticky drink and the trouble makers tried to run. Their shoes were quite stuck to the tiles, so that when they lifted their feet, they made a squelching, sucking sound. This caused them to become apoplectic with glee, even Rosie had a hard time trying to keep a straight face.

"No. Changed my mind. You can all stay here and clean up every surface. And you'll have to make do with Mr Kiplings." she said. Then turned and dragged herself out of the kitchen.

"It was worth it." Celia gasped, reaching for a mop, her feet like glue. And the lads agreed. "But my dad'd go mad if I did anything like that." Niall announced.

Later, after doing the rounds again with more tea and cupcakes, Rosie flopped onto the settee for a nap. But troubled recollections of Clare hindered her rest. ' Should she confront her brother and give him what for? Perhaps she ought to have a chat with Dan later.' and comforted, Rosie drifted into sleep.

It was dusk, the air was full of birdsong, a pleasant breeze carried the sweet smell of wheat and fragments of chaff from off the fields and the sky was a deep navy with slashes of pink. But Bethany was heedless to the rituals of harvest. She was sneaking into one of the sheds for a joint and an update on the school scandals. She settled herself on a wooden crate and, glancing round the breezy twilit space, fished out her phone, hoping she would get a signal in the confined space.

"So, how did Leavesley get on at the club? Did they get in?"

"Seems like it."

"Shit. And did they all get cocktails?"

The click of the shed door locking made Bethany jump. She fumbled through the gloom to call "Who's there" and give the door a push with her shoulder.

"Fuck it Jules. This shed door's locked. I'm trapped in here. That'll be my smart arse of a brother and his new best mates. I'd better go. I've got to try and figure a way out."

"Why don't you ring your mum?"

"I can't. None of them have mobiles and I don't know the number of the cottage. Anyway she'd only start asking what I'm doing in here. Keep me updated. Bye." Bethany stumbled round the wheelbarrows, tools and mowers looking for loose boards she could squeeze through but ended up only rattling the door again and staring at a tiny window, only twelve inches in depth. She scrambled carefully up onto a potting table, willing it not to collapse. Then pushing herself up until she lay horizontally in the narrowest of gaps, she started to force her body through. 'I hope this doesn't do any damage to my boobs' she thought as she turned her head sideways and saw her breasts flattened against the window frame. It looked like a child could not fit but bit by bit she wormed through and fell outside, landing on her side on a pile of bricks stacked under the window. Cursing, rubbing her sore breasts and limping, Bethany furiously went in search of the two boys and their female ringleader.

Round the corner of the shed, the brown bear of a dog slunk off into the field. Celt knew instinctively she would be in deep trouble if the girl had spotted her leaning on the outside of the shed door.

It was a bit of a hike and he wouldn't have ventured on such a trek for any other reason, but John had found the real ale pub. Favouring real ale pubs helped to kid himself that he was a connoisseur of fine ales rather than admitting to be the alcoholic he was. Really, he resented the extortionate cost of chemical free, organic or local beer, couldn't care less about that or the taste. It was escapism and losing his inhibitions he craved. He thought he was amusing and entertaining when drunk, did not consider that he was rude, crude and obnoxious during his journey into the oblivion he sought.

Ivy trailed the white stucco walls up to the creaking 'The Black Horse' sign. Stone mounting blocks and a round studded oak door spoke of earlier times, of yeomen stiffly swinging off big old nags, of sheepdogs lying patiently in the porch and red cheeked old men stepping unsteadily out into the black and cold starry night, to stagger down unlit lanes to their cottages. John stood, seemingly admiring the exuberant hanging baskets draped over the windows but really he was savouring the day long drinking session ahead. He stepped over two dogs stretched out on the porch and sighed with pleasure once in the bar, he was home. Other early morning drinkers shuffled around, pints held lovingly in their hands in a cheery, meaningless discourse. Later the pub would fill with couples coming in to take advantage of the two meals for the price of one for seniors offer but food was not the aim of this brotherhood. John sat on a hard wooden bench and smiled indulgently over his pint at the rowdy group by the bar. Occasionally he would add comments to their witless gossip until, finally he wheedled himself into their circle. These men were his breed, the rambling drunken exchanges, his school. They swapped tales of cars breaking down en-route to the coast, then quickly selling them on returning home before their faults could manifest. Or how, in their day, they used to boast to young women of their exploits as drummers in semi-professional bands, or describe the brilliant way, as barristers, they had won a case for a grateful client. Then, they would scoff at the women's naivety. He recalled the nights he used to take young women home when his wife was at work. Until the hilarious time she came home ill and discovered a woman in the marital bed. Or how, after a night at the casino and unable to find his way home, he slept it off in a doorway and told his ex he had worked all night. Oh, what an entertaining fellow he became. Until, over consumption of alcohol and lack of food forced him to retire quietly to his table.

Just before time was called, there was a series of strangled cries from somewhere in the centre of the circle of men, a body slid down amongst the legs and a grey face could be seen amongst the collective feet. On which, there was an incoherent exchange between them. Then, manhandling the poor chap to a corner, the men propped him on a stool, leaning him against the wall. They then shuffled back to the bar and more subdued than before, continued their conversation.

A young couple were watching from the nook. They stared in alarm, glanced at one another and then hurried over to the sick man.

"You're not going to leave him like that?" the young man called to the group.

"He's alright. He can't hold his ale, that's all."

The young woman was taking his pulse and lifting his eyelids.

"He's not alright. He's hardly got a pulse. I'm getting an ambulance." She ran to the bar, asked to use the phone and spoke urgently into it.

The barman now looked alarmed. He joined the young woman to see if she needed any help.

"Let's take him into the snug and lay him on his side" and the three of them half dragged, half lifted the dead weight into the quiet snug. The barman hurried upstairs for blankets.

The old timers at the bar were muttering angrily to themselves now, putting on coats in readiness to leave. John was unsure, he really wanted to flee but he also felt a bit queasy and the barman had disappeared, so couldn't get him a taxi.

The door burst open and two paramedics rushed in on a gust of fresh air, lugging their magic life saving bags, two border collies trotting behind them, looking round the room for their masters.

"He's in there" an elderly woman said quietly.

Now the pub was silent, subdued. The old timers left. John nursed his whisky, his 'nightcap'. 'This was a nuisance. He wondered if the elderly couple had a mobile phone, it was unlikely but it probably wasn't a good idea to go to the bar. He could then ring Simon and get him to pick him up. It was 11.30, surely he wouldn't be out, would he? Well, he'd be back by now if he was.'

John approached the couple, who were trying not to glance towards the drama in the snug but were clearly concerned.

Suddenly the atmosphere had become thoughtful, respectful, allowing the sufferer his dignity. So, when John approached and asked if the couple would ring his brother it seemed such an indiscretion. Reluctantly they handed him the phone and reluctantly Simon agreed to fetch him. Then, rather than risk witnessing any more unpleasantness, John stepped outside and leaned unsteadily on a tree until his brother swung into the car park and beckoned angrily at him.

The last thing that Simon needed was having to step outside again. It had been a busy day, he was knackered and was about to go to bed. The golf course had proven to be challenging and required him to spend several hours in the clubhouse bar to recover. Luckily his fellow players were an entertaining bunch and he participated in supping some fine ales and whiskies. Being over the limit, he drove very steadily back to the cottage, just in time for Clare's rather good chicken casserole. It was a peaceful evening, the kids had gone up to their rooms after dinner and he settled on the settee to catch up on an episode of Between the Lines. Even Clare had retired, complaining it was too violent but he was not going to watch that rubbish 'French and Saunders' was he? At home Clare would retire to the bedroom so she could watch her not funny shows from the bed. Simon hauled his trainers back on, grabbed his quilted jacket off the peg and hurried out the front door. He was oblivious to the white ghost of a barn owl gliding to a horse chestnut, its shriek eerie in the silence. 'What a bloody nuisance his brother was. He'd always asked favours of him, usually regarding money. Could he borrow £100 for this month's payment on that stupid little sports car he was so ridiculously proud of. Could Simon just see him right for this month's rent on his flat? Of course he never got any of his money back. Then there were the items, 'could he borrow the sit on mower to help the old guy across the road who struggled to mow his orchard?'

It just didn't ring true. John had never been known for his good deeds. A set of drills, an outdoor music centre, his spare barbecue, and not one of them returned. Simon suspected he had sold them but could not bring himself to challenge his brother. Simon took it upon himself to be head of the family and, as such, needed to cover up his brother's indiscretions, for he knew the reason for John's behaviour. Growing up he had witnessed some of the punishments his father had inflicted on the cuckoo in the nest, the leather belt across his brother's backside, the women folk in the family fussing and spoiling him one moment then chastising him the next, shutting him away if visitors came. He had been spared such treatment, yet both boys accepted it. It was Rosie who stood up to their parents, who stood in front of John when the belt came out, who called out for justice on his behalf and who was sent to her room without food each time. Simon could never bring himself to intervene. He would creep into a corner and play quietly with his toy trucks, hoping his half brother would see this as being supportive and that his father would see it as approval. No one would check on Rosie, who would lie on her bed hungry and furious, willing her mother to disobey the tyrant and come up to kiss her goodnight. But she never did. Later, she was equally as shocked and outraged by John's behaviour but no one took any notice of her. It was always his brother that John summonsed when trouble came calling, he knew his sister would try to counsel him or interfere.

So it was Simon who turned out in a tracksuit in the midnight cold while over the limit. He was curt with his brother but John was used to this, knew that getting his way was worth the price of disapproval. After all, he had suffered disapproval and distaste all his life.

As they pulled into the drive a light went out in Simon and Clare's bedroom and the cottage stood dark and silent, also in cold disapproval.

Sunday

Why are you late for Lunch?

Celia was lying in wait, hidden in a dusty old broom cupboard in the murky silence of the upstairs corridor, a lace bonnet of cobwebs over her hair. She was fighting off a sneeze while struggling with her costume in the dark. At a sound on the stairs she peered through the keyhole. Two figures were chattering their way towards the cupboard and to her joy, they had not flicked the light on. She waited, she held her nerve, until the blurred silhouettes had gone past and then, with a tiny wail, she floated as best as she could, out of the cupboard.

Ewan and Niall turned at the eerie sound to see a figure, white in the gloom, rush down the corridor towards the stairs. Niall couldn't stop his scream "What the hell?" he had grabbed Ewan's arm and was pulling him.

Ewan snorted. "It's alright. Its my bloody sister."

"But it was all white."

Ewan snapped a light on. "She's got a sheet over her. She's bonkers. Take no notice."

He grinned. "You never know what's next with her."

Celia appeared on the stairs and casually sauntered past.

"Hi fellas. What's up Niall. You look like you've seen a ghost."

"Told you!" Ewan stopped his sister. "Now what makes you think that, sis?"

"Oh I don't know. He just looks a bit pale and jumpy."

"Funny. That's just how you looked in that sheet."

"Wouldn't I look brown if I was in shit?" She scoffed.

"Ha Ha. I gather you're bored already Celia?"

Suddenly the cat streaked up the corridor with the grinning brown dog lolopping in pursuit. They shot between the children's legs, into one of the bedrooms, then out again and down the stairs.

"Dad's going to explode" Niall looked alarmed.

"Only if he finds out," Celia said. "She won't hurt your cat. She's never caught anything yet and if they turn on her she's terrified. She's a wuss. Eh, why don't we go and explore all those sheds outside?"

The two lads looked at each other, "Good idea."

At that moment Rosie padded out of the bathroom, aromatic steam escaping out behind her. A grass green towel curved around her, damp hair in dark tendrils over her bare shoulders. She made a shower look an exotic practice.

"It's cold on this landing. The soap in there is jasmine and patchouli, reminds me of my teenage years."she informed them as she hurried past.

Then abruptly stopped and observed them sceptically from over her shoulder, eyes narrowing. "What are you three up to?"

"Nothing mum." Ewan flung his arm round Niall.

But Rosie's antennae was up. "Celia, why are you lugging a sheet around?"

"Ewan wet himself and he didn't want anyone to know, so I was just going to hang it out on the line to dry." Celia replied sweetly.

"I did not then." Ewan shouted.

"It's alright. That sometimes happens when you first sleep in a strange bed." Rosie offered her most reassuring voice. "I'll check the mattress, don't you worry about it Ewan."

"Mum." Ewan called but she had stepped into the bedroom. 'Already telling dad probably.' he thought, then turned his attention to his sister, who was already racing towards the stairs.

"Come on slowcoach." she challenged from over her shoulder.

And he chased after the torment and grinning Niall as they slid down the bannister. Simon was about to pick up the Daily Mail from a side table in the hallway.

"Niall, what are you up to?"

Niall raced to the front door before he answered. "It's called fun, dad." And the giggling trio ran into the sunshine.

Later, as the Hunter family headed for the kitchen just nicely in time for breakfast, they could hear a terrible racket coming from the conservatory.

"What's going on?" Grace asked, stepping behind John for protection. "It sounds like somebody's being attacked. Oh dear, what can it be?" Her voice quavered.

"Now you stay here mother. John and I will have a look." Simon pushed his mother behind the settee and indicated for John to follow. They crept towards the closed glass door from where shouts, screams, an excited barking of a dog and yes, laughter seeped into the lounge. The men stared into the conservatory, then Simon thrust the door violently open.

"What the hell is going on?" he shouted in.

The Morris family all stopped and looked up. They were all rolled into a large ball, legs and arms sticking out, half in, half out the french windows, Ewan complaining loudly that the steps were digging in his back. From somewhere in the jumble, Celia's arm stuck out so she could hit him on the head. On the bottom, with everyone piled on, lay Dan, red faced and out of breath, trying to extricate himself while tickling Celia with a large feather. You could hear her giggling from somewhere in the centre. Rosie, curled up in a position that looked impossible, was busy nipping Dan's bottom with finger and thumb and shouting for Sapphire to help her, he was busy getting free. But Sapphire was bent over the other side of the sphere, her spine curved back, laughing helplessly as the ball rolled right down the final steps and onto the lawn, the frantic dog barking and chasing it, then leaping on top. This caused so much mirth that the people ball unwound and became individuals lying exhausted on their backs, staring up at the sun. At one side stood Niall watching in amazement, not sure whether to laugh or look as furious as his dad.

"What the hell is going on?" Simon repeated to the now horizontal group.

"It's called a play fight Simon. You should try it one day." Dan called.

The kids were now subdued into mere giggling and Niall joined in. Even John smirked and a relieved Grace assured Simon that 'no harm was done' as she stepped away from the back of the settee, her features relaxed. "Rosie, you should have more dignity."

Rosie sniggered. "Oh come on, let's finish getting breakfast ready Dan." she stood up, brushing grass and soil off her jeans. "God forbid we should have some fun."

No-one noticed Clare's sad face watching from the doorway as she realized what she was missing, how wonderful family life could be.

"If you keep piling all this food onto us Rosie we're going to be blimps by the time we leave" John sat back from the kitchen table and lit up his cigar.

"Feel free to do a more frugal breakfast for us tomorrow John." Dan responded, looking meaningfully at Rosie cleaning all the remnants of the full English off the table and passing dirty plates to Clare at the dishwasher. John shrugged and rubbed at a dollop of tomato sauce hanging on the edge of his shirt, threatening to plop between the buttons and onto his belly.

"Can you put this shirt in to wash when you're doing a load, sis?"he asked. The group all glanced at Rosie, her face was a picture. It was with great effort she only responded with "No, do it yourself."

Celt, meanwhile, was hoovering up all the crumbs under the table, next to Celia who was tying her brother's shoelaces together. The cat, safely up high on the cupboard was delicately eating bits of bacon from his dish.

"So, what is everyone doing today?" Rosie asked, grabbing a stack of plates as they started to slide off the draining board.

Simon got up from the table. "We have to pay for any breakages you know."

"Well, I would like to take my family out for lunch" an imperious but quavering voice spoke up and Grace struggled to stand, "My treat."

The others looked at each other. There was a silence.

"Only if we eat at the pub." John stated.

Bethany scowled. "I couldn't possibly eat another big meal. I'm watching my weight."

"I was hoping to go walking today." Rosie sounded hesitant.

"I'd love a walk." Clare agreed.

"I'll need you to help me get ready ." Grace said firmly and Clare's face fell.

"I can't eat for ages, we've just had a massive breakfast." Celia groaned and the others all nodded in agreement.

"Oh, go off for your walks then. But I want you all back here for 12.30 to get changed for lunch." the tone of a puppet ruler, a pretence of authority.

Dan glared at Celia as she stuck her tongue out at the back of her Gran's head.

"I thought I might take the kids horse riding if they'd like." Sapphire glanced expectantly at the four youngsters, two of whom started to dance and shout with glee, while Bethany and Niall stood in silent horror.

"I am Not going horse riding." Bethany stated.

"I'd sooner go to the dentist." Niall agreed.

"Fair enough." Sapphire was undeterred. "You stop here and you two hurry and get ready, we've got to be back in three hours."

"I hope you'll be back. All of you. I don't want to be let down." Grace tried to stand up with dignity but the chair legs were caught on the rug. Ewan and Celia rushed to pull the chair back and support their grandma so she didn't fall backwards. "Thank you dears."

"They'll all be back mother. Or they'll have me to answer to." Simon took his paper and coffee to the armchair. "Are you going to help mother pick her clothes, Clare?"

Clare looked crestfallen. "I really want to go a walk." Her face remained impassive but a pulse began to thump in her hand and she quickly picked up a magazine so no-one spotted the shake.

Simon was taken by surprise at his wife's dissent, covering his confusion with a warning lift of the eyebrow and a second reminder that his mother would need help. Even as Clare's head went down and she started to shuffle towards the stairs Rosie spoke up.

"No, she's coming a walk with me." she asserted.

"So, who's going to help mother?" Simon looked up from his paper in annoyance.

"Well, you could." Rosie replied.

Simon snorted. "I don't think so."

"Of course he can't. "Grace said hurriedly. "It'll wait till you get back Clare. I'm going to sit and talk to my son now while I finish this coffee ." She carried her cup, rattling alarmingly in its saucer, over to the armchair.

"I hope that's John you mean, because I'm going to have five minutes peace and quiet with my paper."

At Simon's words, Grace did a turn around, trying to look nonchalant. "Where is John?"

"He's reading his paper in the garden, so he won't want you disturbing him either." Simon calmly said.

Grace stood still, confused and unable to move. At the sight of her trembling lip, Rosie and Clare both hurried over.

"Come on mum. Take no notice of that nasty man. We'll quick help you sort your outfit out before we go our walk." Rosie glared at Simon, who stared back unconcerned and the two women took Grace's arm to help her up the stairs.

Simon watched the three women as they left the room, Ewan rushing to open the door for them. He was not happy with the friendship that was flourishing between his wife and sister. If Rosie started filling Clare's head with defiant ideas it could cause trouble in their marriage. He would have to try and keep them apart. Just that morning Clare had assured him she had not seen the gossipy or calculating side of Rosie he had told her about, nor the nastiness towards their mother. He had countered that his sister was just trying to gain her confidence before reeling her in but Clare had just given him a strange look.

"I'll give you lot a lift if you like." Dan suggested to Sapphire. "I don't want to stay here." he flicked his head towards Simon.

"Thanks Dad, that'd be great. I was going to ask if I could drive the old Ford but I didn't think you'd be keen." Laughing, Sapphire headed for the stairs.

"I should think not. You've not passed your test yet, young lady." Dan called.

"I'll just get my old jeans on. I can't wait to see you on a horse." she responded.

"I'm not riding." Dan was alarmed.

"Of course not." came an unconvincing response from upstairs.

The house was peaceful for a while and Simon settled down with his Daily Mail. Their was a tantalizing headline. 'A historic twelve page picture souvenir of our greatest ever protest march. And with a backdrop of a tide of people carrying No Iraq War banners, Britain tells Blair You're on your own.'

Grace, banished to her bedroom, was worrying whether she may have to take charge with the meal because she was paying. That had always been Harry's responsibility when he was alive. She began to worry about all the possible embarrassments that might befall her. 'What if the toilets were upstairs? A fall in front of other diners, the youngsters getting loud, or worse, Bethany having a tantrum, Rosie and Dan wearing their outlandish, totally inappropriate outfits. How much of a tip nowadays.' But she could not face her worst fears, John and Simon's bad behaviour, it hurt too much. Better to make excuses for them.

Bethany too was in her room sorting out her outfit. She had made contact with a man from London who also happened to be on holiday in the Lakes. He was willing to drive to Keswick later that afternoon so Bethany could have a spin in his Golf GTI, an older but still fast model, 'much like himself', he quipped. She was glad that Niall had been persuaded to go riding with them, it meant the little creep wouldn't be pestering her. Stretching on the bed she admired her reflection in the wardrobe mirror as the sunlight danced across her face and she studied the room for the first time.

'This might not turn out to be such a bad holiday after all,' she reflected. Even though the cottage was twee, the furnishings ancient and the company unbearable. The oak bed was huge and soft with a lemon and grey eiderdown and blankets and bolster pillows rather than a duvet. Secretly she found this endearing and romantic, almost other wordly. An oak washstand housed an elegant bowl decorated with cream and lemon lilies. Various bowls and jugs in the same pattern held yellow and ruby chrysanthemums and cream lilies, their perfume intoxicating. Their were cream and lemon thick Persian rugs scattered round the large, sunlit room with heavy, gold velvet drapes at the full length windows. She surprised herself with the strong urge to get out her watercolours and paint the scene. Perhaps because it represented an earlier, more elegant and contented era, Bethany began to feel calmer, not so angry when in this grand room. Appreciation was not an emotion she was used to but the calmness was like a drug. Her room at home was deep pink and jet, the bed hard and black with a cerise duvet cover, black framed photo's of pop stars all dressed in sparkly tight outfits lined the walls and her black appliances looked functional and rigid. A tough, unforgiving space.

Rosie and Clare had wandered down the hill and discovered a loamy footpath weaving gently into the dim coolness of silent woods. Between the trees, a cloak of vivid bronze, russet and sepia leaves conjured the pungency of autumn. This walk, the women were subdued. Clare, unwilling to spoil the magical peace with worrying thoughts see-sawing in her mind, followed her sturdy companion through the mud, weaving round the trees and felt reassured by her calm spiritual guidance.

But suddenly Rosie stopped to walk alongside.

"Something's been bothering me. Can I ask about it?

Dread swept across Clare's face. "Yes of course." Quietly.

"Did Simon ever talk about me?"

"Not much." Clare looked away to hide the lie.

"He didn't bad mouth me then?" Casually.

"I suppose I got the impression that you two didn't get on."

"So he never told you I was spiteful or that I didn't like you?"

Silence.

"I thought so. It's alright. I know what he's like. He's busy isolating you, you know."

Clare stopped walking, her face weary. "I don't understand. Why would he do that? He's my husband." She watched bleakly as two squirrels chased around the massive girth of an oak. "He loves me." she murmured.

"Yes." Rosie said. "We can talk about it another time, eh?"

Clare nodded, how she wanted to talk but it was as if Simon was behind them, listening in, anticipating her betrayal.

" Let's just enjoy this walk. It's such a bonny morning." said Rosie. "Look at them bloody squirrels!"

This roused Clare out of her doldrums. "Don't you like squirrels? I always think they're so entertaining, so clever."

"Yeah. Especially when you see them going back and forth with the bulbs you've just planted, then digging holes in your lawn to bury them."

"I see what you mean but the way their tails flick up over their bodies. And those black eyes, full of mischief."

Don't forget their strength. When you watch them lugging a bird feeder full of peanuts across the garden."

The two women laughed and Clare was relieved that the Simon topic had been postponed, even though she so wanted to confide in this insightful woman.

They came out of the gloom by the edge of town. Allotments created a backdrop of rust red and yellow, the intermingled shapes of flowers and vegetables. Pumpkins crept across to cabbages, apples rotted on the soil, drunken wasps in their hollows and huge chrysanthemum heads nodded above the ferny tops of carrots. A spectacular pageant staged by the cooperation of humans and nature.

Twelve miles away the map guided the family along winding lanes, zigzagging through bleak and open moorland, the old van spluttered down a farm track towards the riding stables nestled in a valley of gorse and ferns. The girls and Ewan were chatting loudly with excitement but as the van rattled over the cattle grid, passing horses in the fields each side, Niall firmly bit his lip and Dan became silent, his hands gripping the wheel. He had discovered that Sapphire booked him on the outride too and try as he might, he couldn't stop the nerves. He was aware of Niall, his fellow sufferer, glancing forlornly across for reassurance so cast silly, sideways grins across but clearly they were unconvincing as the lad was now quietly groaning and pushing a shakey hand through his hair.

"Should we not bother?" Dan quietly asked him through clenched teeth. "She can't make us." So relieved, they both relaxed a bit. Hesitantly Dan spoke firmly and yet casually to Sapphire. "Niall and I aren't going to bother. We're just going to have a bit of a stroll round the farm."

"Sorry dad. Once it's booked we have to pay whether you ride or not. Apparently they used to get a lot of people not turning up."

"I wonder why." Dan muttered. "Listen that's alright, I'll still pay." He was hopeful.

"This is an early birthday present from me. You need to try new experiences."

Dan sighed, it was hopeless. He looked resolutely across to his companion who just shrugged miserably.

Once at the farm, the friendly lecture in the tack room about the importance of the right size riding hat in case you should get tossed off and land on your head and how to make sure you keep control of your horse at all times didn't help neither. ' After all, those buggers know a soft touch when they get one on their backs' the teenage girl quipped unhelpfully. When a black horse the size of a wall came striding out of the stable and was halted at the side of Dan he refused to get on and Niall cried quietly as he was hitched up onto the back of a lively pinto pony. Ewan climbed confidently onto the mounting block and swung onto a pretty grey. The girls both asked for 'something lively' and two white Arab ponies were led out of the stables, snorting and sashaying across the yard. The horses started to move away leaving Dan to face his monster of a Shire horse, slow and gentle, it placidly stared him in the eye as it finished chewing its oats.

"Come on dad, get on." urged Celia over her shoulder.

"You can do it." laughed Sapphire.

"My horse is moving" called Niall "Make it stop."

"You have to make it stop," the slight, teenage instructress told him but she moved over to put her horse next to his. Niall hoped his suspicion that she wouldn't have the strength to stop a running hamster was false.

"Do you want to be on a lead rein dad?" Celia sniggered, her horse dancing sideways across the yard.

Dan's pride took over and he struggled off the mounting block and onto the broad back just as the guide made clicking noises and they ambled through the gate onto the open moors. Dan groaned. The Arabs needed no encouragement and rearing up, took off at a canter, the girls whooping with joy and the grey pony surging forward to catch up.

"Keep those ponies under control" the sixteen year old called. "We'll just take a nice sedate stroll for now" she told a relieved Dan and Niall.

It was a hazy, balmy day and the horses strolled sedately along the trail behind the girl, also sat atop a mad side prancing Arab. Bees were flushed out of the scented gorse as the horse's legs brushed past and buzzed upwards, carrying their loads of pollen away. Dan found the steady rhythm hypnotic, the sun on his back and the hills ahead. Niall also had stopped crying and though one hand clung to the pummel, he began to look at his surroundings. Their guide was unconcernedly telling them about the landscape as she danced sideways beside them. The crazy group were already at the bottom of the hill and turning to gallop back up to them.

So Dan felt relaxed as the group plodded into the cool twilight of a wood. His horse led the way down a leaf strewn path as he breathed in the new smells of mud and leaf mould. But the girl led the others down another path and casually called to Dan to turn his horse round.

"How do I do that?" he asked calmly.

"Just pull on the rein one side."

The group stopped and waited but Billy plodded on. Dan now started to feel the first twinges of alarm. "He won't turn.",

"Where are you going dad?" Celia called as the horse's large rump meandered its way downwards between the trees.

"Turn the rein and kick him gently the same side, he'll turn." the girl shouted down the hill.

"He isn't taking any notice." came faintly back.

"I'll fetch him." said Celia and kicking her Arab, she was raised into the air, then bolted forward.

"No. No. Billy doesn't like your horse" the instructor called but it was too late, Celia was whooping 'to the rescue' to her dad, who was twisting round in his saddle in supplication as the group watched from between the trees at the top of the hill. Out of the corner of his eye the placid Billy saw the white devil hurtling towards him and sternly stepped up his pace.

"We seem to be going faster." Dan sounded alarmed now.

"Bring Sparky back" the young leader called "Billy hates him." She was trying not to sound alarmed too but now both riders were out of earshot.

Suddenly Billy took off at a speed that belied his bulk. Dan screamed and clung onto his mane.

"Coming dad. We'll soon stop him, hang on." Celia kicked her horse who swerved and plunged between the trees. Dan was chanting obscenities into Billy's ear now, his knees clinging and knocking against the horse's flanks. But his powerful legs pumping and white eyed, he watched the pony catching up behind. Suddenly they were alongside, Celia, cowgirl style, lying along the side of her pony ready to grab the dangling rein. But Billy saw and swerved into the bushes off the path, a tree branch swept Dan backwards off the horse and with an 'Oomph' he was sprawled on his back in the mud. Celia meanwhile, with a huge effort and reach, had grabbed Billy's rein, he decided he was in enough trouble and promptly slid to a stop. Celia found herself hurtling in the air across to Billy, crashing into his side. He looked at her in disdain as she slid down his side, then wandered off towards a lush clump of grass. Dan watching from his soft bed of mud screamed again as Celia disappeared beneath the hooves of two horses. Then Billy wandered off giving him a clear vantage of his daughter, also flat on her back and shrieking with laughter"Are you alright?" she managed to ask as the others arrived.

They caught the horses, stood the hapless pair up covered in mud, with Dan bleeding from a nasty gash on his leg.

"We'd better call it a day and get you bandaged up." the girl nodded to Dan. "What a relief. I thought you'd both come croppers."

"I think we both did come croppers, didn't we?" Dan said.

"Well, your leg's facing the right way." the girl replied, "Unlike the young lad last year."

"I don't want to hear anymore. Let's go." Dan hobbled to his horse. "Can someone help me get back on this thing? And you'd better behave yourself." He looked Billy sternly in the eye, before being shoved back up onto his back in a most ungainly fashion. "I'm going back to the stables now." Dan determinedly turned Billy towards the edge of the woods. "Now you follow me and ride like a sensible young woman Celia. Grace is going to have a field day."

Billy sedately took Dan, ripped jeans flapping and trying to look as dignified as he could, back to the stables.

At the dot of twelve, Rosie and Clare, both slightly flushed from rushing back from their walk, escorted Grace down the stairs with a sense of occasion. The old woman had fussed and deliberated for so long neither of them had time to change.

"Couldn't you have made an effort?" Simon said to Clare as he sat his mother on the front seat. But Rosie had heard.

"She's been too busy helping Your mother." and then countered. "I notice you don't say anything to him." She tossed her head towards John, his stomach bulging between the shirt buttons and shiny black trousers belted beneath. They all sat in silence in the car, waiting for Bethany, who finally sauntered over talking on her phone, unconcerned. She was wearing a low cut top and shorts and heavy make up. Rosie watched, bemused as the girl struggled to open the door with her long, deep pink plastic nails. Grace tutted but said nothing, it would not please her son and what would be the point? Bethany took no notice of her either.

"Budge up." She shoved her mother with her hip as she sat.

"There's not a lot of room and I don't know, is that's suitable?" Clare suggested hesitantly. "It's cold today." she added, without conviction.

"Oh mother, give up." Bethany responded and Grace was reminded of Simon at that age. She would liked to have told this young madam how rude she was but remained tight lipped.

"Don't start Clare. " Simon said. "She's only jealous." he called to the girl, who sniggered back.

Rosie, squashed in the back space, opened her mouth to shout to Simon what a foolish thing to say to an impressionable teenager but Grace had swung round from the front seat, her stare imploring her to keep quiet. So Rosie firmly closed her mouth again and concentrated on keeping her balance as the car bounced over the gravel drive.

The hotel, once grand and elegant but now shabby and outdated, was on the now pedestrianized High Street, the cheap, modern hotels by the motorway having had much to do with its demise. Rosie knew the food was going to be poor and over priced. Grace walked in the lobby with as much dignity as her arthritis would allow and strutted down the wide staircase hoping it wasn't obvious she was clinging to the wooden balustrade, but gliding elegantly, the 1940's starlet she imagined in her mind's eye. She commandeered her family to their table and addressed the waitresses in her poshest telephone voice.

"The rest of our family will be with us shortly." Grace waved her hand towards the empty seats. "Perhaps we could see your wine list in the meantime" and then waved the staff imperiously away. Then to her family, in a strong Nottingham dialect, "Where are they? I knew this'd 'appen."

"Oh mother, don't fret." Simon told her. "We'll order our dinners. It's their loss if they're not here, I'm not waiting around."

"I don't think it would hurt to order a drink and give them a bit of leeway." Rosie told him, shocked.

The staff had made an effort but it was obvious that morale was low. Their white shirts and black skirts were as outdated as the red napkins and murky wine glasses, The tablecloths were yellowy white and holey, the carpet a dizzy mix of 1960s colours and patterns that clashed with the red flock wallpaper. Only polished walnut panelling suggested an earlier, more distinguished era.

Secretly, Rosie was worried. She always worried when Celia or Sapphire embarked on one of their crazy ideas. Both of them were impulsive and adventurous and both had suffered injuries because of it. Sapphire had joined several charity excursions, breaking her arm on a bike ride across the Gobi desert, getting malaria while helping to build wells in Africa and nearly getting swept out to sea when coasteering in Wales. They were the ones that Rosie had found out about and now Celia, already with several open water swims and marathons under her belt, was coming up to the age to want to go off too. Rosie groaned to herself, hoping the girls weren't trying any heroics on horseback.

But it was Dan who came limping in to the dining room, who had a rip in the knee of his jeans and bandages around his hand and leg. He was supported by Celia one side and Sapphire the other, the lads chattering behind.

"Oh no." Rosie ran to him."What happened?"

"Billy had a mind of his own" Dan looked sheepish.

"I didn't think you were even riding."Rosie tried not to laugh, then a stern look across as she spotted the two girls smirking. "Are you alright?"

"Neither did I. Them two put me up to it." He tossed his head towards the girls with an 'Ouch'.

The youngsters could contain it no longer. they all burst out laughing.

"It was the standard cowboy movie mum." Ewan snorted. "We were galloping along the path, dad's horse veered off, he'd lost control completely and he got swept off its back by an overhanging branch."

"Will you lot be quiet and come and sit down, you're late." Grace called. "I might have known you'd spoil my lunch. And you need to go and clean up Dan." Dan was just limping past."Sorry Grace. Don't mind me. I'll just hobble to the bathroom." He continued his slow trajectory to the toilets.

"Mum, he couldn't help it." Rosie was mad.

Grace stuck to her guns. "Well, a man of his age shouldn't be horse riding."

During the meal Rosie's fears were confirmed. Celia had also fallen off her horse trying to rescue her dad. The uncles weren't interested, Grace censured the girl's stupidity but Rosie felt a mixture of pride and fear for her daughter's foolhardiness. For a blinding moment she imagined the parade of possible accidents and subsequent injuries that could befall her daughter in the coming years, but the waitress arrived with her overcooked roast and broke the spell.

Her mother was holding court, she had half raised herself out of the chair, her dinner forgotten. 'Her parents couldn't afford the luxury of riding lessons, while the youth of today took the travelling, the partying and the unlimited spending for granted.' Rosie refrained from asking her if she would have liked to have seen her granddaughter leaving school at fourteen to be sent out to work, so their father could drink all his wages down the Red Lion, as she had?

John meanwhile, from his seat at the end of the table was becoming more loquacious as several pints took effect, interrupting the matriarch to regale his trapped audience with riveting stories from his pub life. The win at table tennis in the bar of Soleil Hotel, Minorca 1978. The best score at Long Eaton rifle range, April 1986. A rosette and a brace of pheasants for being best beater for his farmer friend, 1991. 'Drunk of the Year' award for his exceptional score of six whiskies and twelve pints in The Black Horse, June 2008.

"Those poor birds." was all Sapphire could say.

Simon oversaw the lunch, scolding the staff for bringing his mother's dinner last and putting her in a draughty spot. Neither had they offered him the wine to taste before serving it. Meanwhile, he reminded

Grace not to talk with her mouth full and she couldn't possibly need the toilet yet, while at the same time beckoning Clare to take her. Seeing the beaten look on her mother in law's face, Clare glared at her husband, helped Grace out of her chair and complimented her on her gracious outfit. But it was no good. It was not Clare's affection and approval Grace was looking for but her two sons. Sadly, it was not to be. The two patriarchs had no respect for the women and interrupted or criticized them without conscience. Rosie could hardly bear to watch this game she had grown up with. She cast a grateful glance at her beloved partner, his face still smeared with mud and his wild hair flopping around his eyes. He sensed her stare and broke off from his story telling with the boys to blow her a kiss. Niall was in a new world of horse riding adventures and fantasy creatures with Ewan and felt happy. Bethany carefully picked her way through her lasagne, not wanting to mess up her make up. Then, while puddings were being decided, she announced she was going to look round the town, collected her phone, bag and coat and marched across the dining room.

"Don't you want a dessert, there's your favourite, treacle sponge?" Simon called.

"No thanks."

"How long will you be?" Clare was alarmed. "We don't want to go back to the house and then have to come out again Bethany."

"I'll find my own way back." And she was gone.

"We don't even know where she's going, let alone when she'll get back." Clare worried. "I bet she doesn't know where the bus station is and it'll be a Sunday service." "Oh stop fussing Clare." Simon bossed. "She'll get a taxi, won't she. They let Their daughter hitch hike up and down the country." He nodded towards Rosie.

"Sapphire is sensible." Dan retorted. "And older."

"Are you suggesting that Bethany isn't?" There was a telling silence around the table, only the boys' intense chat continued.

Grace felt her nerves coming on. She heard different versions of this conversation at home. She knew Bethany was spoilt, that her dad indulged her, that they all ignored Clare, the one with common sense. "That girl will do what she wants." was all she said.

"Did you know that Gran was a very accomplished pianist?" Sapphire tried to steer the conversation into safer waters.

At least these kids are a bit different to the molly coddled pair I have to put up with." Grace thought, then berated herself with 'Comparisons are odious.'

"Don't set her off on that tack," Simon replied. "We'll never hear the end of it." And his mother, who had come to life again, sat back, crushed.

"I think we'd better pay the bill." Rosie said briskly. "I'd like to go back to the house."

Grace immediately nudged Simon's knee under the table, giving him meaningful looks.

"What is it mother?" he responded irritated, then realized and took the envelope of money she passed under the table.

"I'll get the bill." he stated grandly.

Grace felt deflated. After all, this was her day and already the family were letting her down, it's not like she often made demands on them but the lunch had not gone as she had hoped. She wished that her children and their families would all have amiable conversations, enjoying each other's company and that she would be given the opportunity to tell them about her life, such as it was, her own childhood, her dreams and ambitions, that once she she had been a romantic, full of joy and optimism. Then, maybe they might understand she wasn't always a bitter old woman. But she was running out of time. There was a tear in her eye as Clare wrapped her shawl round her shoulders and gave her a hug, whispering 'Take no notice' as Simon swept past them.

"Now where's John gone?" he said, annoyed.

"He's in the bar" Dan said drily.

"He'll have to find his own way back then, I'm not a taxi service."

Sapphire hooked her arm in her Gran's. "Thank you grandma, that was a lovely lunch. " she said, then glanced guiltily at her half eaten cottage pie just being carried away by the waitress. "When we get back, I'd love you to tell Celia all about what you were telling me, you know, when you were growing up, your piano lessons and stuff."

Grace brightened "You don't want to hear an old woman wittering on."

"Yes we do Gran" the girls said in unison.

"I'd like to hear about it too" Clare added. "We only seem to talk about what clothes you want to wear and what to eat when we're at home"

It was getting dusk as the car smoothly climbed the hill and the lights of Cloud cottage came into view. Rosie felt warmer towards her mother than she had done in years and decided to try and see more of Clare now that she had seen how difficult life was for this lovely woman, even though she had eluded Rosie's attempts at friendship in the past. Little did Rosie know how much of a prediction this was. Wedged beside her, Clare was quietly worrying about her daughter, both her safety and her behaviour. Rosie's kids seemed so affectionate, so respectful towards their parents, while Bethany was so spoiled and Niall heading that way. It gave her some comfort to know it was not her doing, yet unfairly, she bore the brunt of her family's ugly behaviour. The old Ford chugged behind, the children full up and sleepy, quietly staring out, Dan concentrating on the winding lane, trying to drown out the drone of John's slurred voice as he described a road trip to Northumberland in his sports car.

Meanwhile, the Diva in question was sat in a black car beside a man who certainly looked a good deal older than the 23 years he had told her he was. 'Uglier too' she thought. It was true about the Golf GTI though and Bethany tried not to look alarmed as he whipped it round the one track lanes, mud and leaves flying up around them. She knew what sort of guy he was. He had not asked anything about herself yet she had already been told about his enthralling life as a D.J. in the trendy bars of London and the night that Fat Boy Slim had approached his set to thrust his business card onto the speaker. In response the word 'Liar' was playing on a loop in Bethany's head. She switched off, she'd heard it all before, wondered if he was admiring her legs. Unusually, this last thought gave her an unbidden jolt of alarm. 'Where was he taking her? She was not used to feeling unsure of herself but away from her friends and home streets, racing round strange lanes not knowing where to with a stranger, she was scared. Despite his black suit and white cuffs, Adam had a seedy look about him. The bald spot she saw when he leaned forward, the crooked and gapped teeth did not match the photograph in his letter. And there was a distinct smell of sour milk in the car, a spilt baby bottle, she guessed. Married with kids. And still he wouldn't say where he was taking her. Bethany's stomach lurched in fear, she was not used to a situation being out of her control. She had been careless and now there was only one thing for it. As the car lurched towards a hamlet of old cottages Bethany spoke up.

"You'll have to pull over. I need a pee."

"There's nowhere to go round here." The man indicated the fenced off fields and open lane.

"Look, if you don't want me to soak your leather seat."

He hurriedly pulled over, Bethany leapt out and ran straight into the front garden of the first cottage in the row and hammered on the door.

The stranger revved up, glared and swore as he drove past then disappeared over the brow of the hill. An elderly woman came to the door and Bethany asked if she could use her house phone as her mobile had no signal and she needed to get her father to pick her up.

“I’m not a bit surprised. There’s very little reception round here thanks to these mountains looming up around us. Not very many people even bother to have one of those devices.” The woman glanced at her Siemens S10 with curiousity. She had clearly not seen one before. Then the kindly soul invited her in, to Bethany’s relief. ‘Just in case that creep comes back’ she thought, still shook up. So, in between drinking tea and eating homemade chocolate cake with the old lady smilingly looking on, Bethany rang her dad and asked him to come and fetch her. The woman thought it was a bit odd that the girl seemed distressed beneath her confident manner but kept her own counsel, just once casually asking if all was O.K.

Simon, on the other hand, did not keep his own counsel. He ranted at Bethany all the way back to Cloud Cottage, half an hour drive away. He had missed a good film, he was over the limit and he was not a taxi service. He did not ask the young girl why she was ringing from a stranger’s house in the middle of nowhere. Bethany sat, sullen and mutinuous, in the back. Clare was waiting anxiously in the porch, her dark hair framed by deep pink roses in their last bloom. Relieved, she hugged her daughter and tried to get her to tell them where she had been but Bethany remained silent, just shrugging her shoulders. “Leave me alone, will you.” But her mother sensed fear behind the unresponsive mask and hoped this was the first step towards Bethany’s epiphany.

The cottage got chilly as the seasonal mists came slowly down the hills like a curtain at the end of a vibrant play, so Dan fetched logs and lit a fire. He had become aware that any music his family put on, in whatever room, including their bedrooms, was being replaced. Clannad became Beethoven, E.L.O. became Elgar and Oasis turned into Frank Sinatra. And each time the volume was turned up. So as he moved through room to room he removed the plugs from the stereo system and the radios.

Bethany had escaped up to her room, a noisy and good natured argument over a scrabble word was going on in the corner and curled up in a chair by the window, Clare watched the mighty clouds rolling past. Sapphire, stretched out on the settee, lazily addressed anyone who might be in the room.

"I'm doing a bit of a one woman show on Tuesday night at the pub if anyone's interested in coming along."

"I'll come." Ewan responded.

"Duh. Does the word pub not mean anything to you Ewan?" Celia threw a Scrabble piece at his head.

Rosie looked up from her book. "I'll ask the others but don't be too surprised if they say no. You know, the kids might be able to go though. I'll ring the pub. I thought we might go to a castle tomorrow if everyone else fancies it."

"Where is everyone else?"

"I think they've all gone up for a" Rosie coughed "read."

"So, they're all asleep then."

"Let's make the most of the peace and quiet." And Rosie cast a meaningful glance across the room at the kids.

Upstairs, Bethany was sat on the sill with the casement window open, fanning the smoke from a joint to spiral out towards a sliver of moon beyond the clouds. A muscular breeze forced itself in and swept around her face, promising new encounters and excitement. She could hear John's snores vibrating through the wall and imagined her gran sleeping peacefully beneath her old counterpane. What surprised her was that mother stayed downstairs when dad came up to read the newspaper, she always followed him like a sheep. It was quite disconcerting.

Simon was more than disconcerted, he was annoyed. The newspaper was spread on the bed, open at the business section but he stared blankly at the pages, his mind busy working out what to do about his wife. She had not come upstairs with him as she should but had chosen to stay with the other family, this would require a stern word. Rosie was such a trouble maker, nothing had changed, always sticking up for her mother or John when she was a kid and dad chastized them. He had been tired and was going to have a lie down but he moved restlessly around the room, trying to think how he was going to get Clare on her own to put her in her place without shouting. It would be far too quiet when everyone came to bed. He turned on the T.V., flicked half heartedly through the channels then turned it off again and an idea came into his mind. He would take her for a drive, perhaps a meal at the pub, just the two of them so he could have a word with her. And reassured, Simon took off his trousers and stretched out on the bed.

Monday

The Castle

Everyone had overslept but finally all were gathered round the table in their customary chairs as Rosie, Dan and Clare scuttled round with pots of coffee and tea, dishes of eggs, racks of toast and baskets of croissants, as had become customary too. Only Bethany was missing, her lateness was also customary.

"Sapphy is playing guitar and piano at the Black Horse on Tuesday night if anyone fancies going along and giving her a bit of support." Rosie suggested lightly. Inside, she was tremulous, hoping her family wouldn't let her down and realize it would mean a lot to Sapphire. But of course, the excuses soon came rolling in.

"Oh I don't frequent pubs as you well know." Grace stated.

John waved a dismissive hand towards Rosie "I'm not listening to a night of rowdy punk rubbish. I'm surprised that pub would even book it."

But Simon looked outraged. "What does she think she's doing Rosie?"

"What?" Rosie's lip became a sarcastic sneer.

"Touting herself at a village pub."

Sapphire responded good naturedly. "I often busk uncle Simon. It's good fun, it keeps me practicing and I make a bit of money at the same time."

But Simon continued to address his sister. "Is there nothing your daughter won't do? First she's hitch hiking in the middle of the night and now she's planning to entertain the pub.

Sapphire glanced at Rosie's angry face in alarm. Luckily her dad was by the sink making more tea. Stretched out on the rug, Celt's legs began to twitch to accompany a low key 'Woof', the only sound for a few chilly moments.

"So, you don't think that Sapphire should entertain in the pub then Simon?" The question was hard as steel, a verbal knife edge.

But Simon was unabashed, "Since when have young women entertained a pub full of men. Well, there is a certain sort. But it's not really the done thing, is it sis?"

"Mum, it's alright." Sapphire tried. She wondered how her uncle had got so stuck in the nineteenth century?

"NO. It's not alright. He's got no right to suggest you are....Well, let's see. What are you suggesting? She has no right to assume she can play guitar as good as the guys perhaps? Or is it that her main aim of jamming in the pub is to pick guys up? Have I understood your concerns Simon?" The sarcasm brought a sigh from Grace.

"Can we just enjoy our breakfasts? I'm tired of you two always falling out. I've put up with this since you were tots."

Simon ignored his mother. "I must say I think both your girls seem a little forward to me." He was enjoying himself now he had got a rise out of his sister.

Over at the toaster Clare looked agitated. "Simon, do you have to...." she ventured then stopped.

Celia whistled softly between her teeth as her dad strolled innocently over with a teapot.

"They just don't seem very feminine to be honest."

"I'm delighted to hear that. we're going for feminist rather than feminine nowadays."

"What's up?" Dan asked.

But Simon interrupted, "I wouldn't let my daughter hitchhike as you know. Neither would I want her entertaining a pub full of men. The horse riding is bad enough. Bethany does not meet up with strange men, I wouldn't allow it."

'Pompous ass.' Dan breathed.

The air was loaded as Rosie tried to gather in her anger and Dan looked round bemused.

Niall put down his croissant, a fleeting moment of indecision flew across his face. "She does dad." he chirped up. "She met one yesterday in his car." Crumbs flew out of his mouth and into his tea. Ewan laughed but he was the only one.

"She met a man in his car." Simon was scathing. "What are you talking about?"

"I saw the letter saying where to meet up and his photo." At this moment Bethany came into the room. She looked round, bemused by everyone's stare. "What?"

Clare kept her voice even but her face was working. "Is this true Bethany? Have you been in contact with a man?" Bethany turned on her brother. "You little shit.What were you doing going through my stuff?"

"I was looking for my Marvel comic and the letter was open."

"As if I'd have that."

"Never mind about that," Clare interrupted. "What do you think you are playing at my girl? You're fifteen years old. Who was this man you met? And how did he get in touch with you?"

Bethany glared. "It was just a bloke. I'm all in one piece, aren't I?

She hoped this tack would nip the inquisition in the bud and get her out of this storm.

So with that, she rushed out of the room and stomped up the stairs to her bedroom, slamming the door behind her.

There was an uneasy shuffling round on seats. Rosie, worried that some would change their minds about the castle, that the day would be spoiled with everyone cooped up and bored, suggested they should all nip and get themselves ready and meet back downstairs in ten minutes. Surprisingly, no-one had changed their minds about going to the castle. Everyone was back downstairs and milling round in the hallway when Bethany moodily made her appearance again.

"What's the weather like?"

"Have a look out the window!"

"You'll need more than just that thin jacket Ewan".

"Has anyone seen my phone?" Bethany was searching through the books and magazines on the coffee table.

Clare decided to let sleeping dogs lie for now.

"Your phone is on the shelf above the toilet. Do you even take that thing into the bathroom?"

"Mind your own business."

Rosie and Dan glanced at one another. Clare opened her mouth to remind her daughter to show a little respect and closed it again. Her instincts told her to wait till Bethany might be more responsive and Simon was not around to undermine her but she was desperate to talk to the girl about her risky behaviour.

"We'll have to take the dog."

"Ooh bloody hell. Yes. We can't leave her here all day."

"Bet they don't let dogs in. There's probably deer and stuff."

"She'll have to stay in the car that's all. And you kids will have to nip back and walk her round the car park at some point."

"How did I guess that was coming?"

"You wanted the dog."

"Do we need to take packed lunches do you think?"

"It'll be closing up by the time we get there!"

"You're right. There'll be a tearoom thank goodness."

“Does anyone know how to get to this Muncaster Castle by the way?”

“Yes. The satnav.”

“I’m impressed. You’ve got one of those GPS gadgets.”

“Of course.”

“Of course he would.” sarcasm!

“You’re wearing my sunglasses.”

“I am not then. These are brown.”

“They are my sunglasses.”

“You won’t need them anyway. It’s raining.”

“Oh no, I forgot to bring a brolly.”

“I saw one hanging around here somewhere.”

“Oh come on. Can we just go?”

Finally the families were grouped outside the cars where another exchange began.

Sapphire thought it would be nice to travel in a car with a decent undercarriage and didn’t smell of wet dog for a change, indicating the sports car.

John was not impressed. “You’re not going to sit and strum that bloody guitar all the way are you?”

“No. No guitar. I’ll sit quietly squashed in that tiny back seat. Gran told me she’d love a ride in your sports car. She can be up front with you.”

John did not look happy but said nothing.

"I'm going with Ewan in their van." Niall said firmly.

Bethany was dressed as if she was heading out to a night club, short white skirt and tee shirt, black clinch belt with sequins, thin leather jacket. Her mother knew she would be frozen but there was no point in saying anything, it would only mean a vicious response from her husband and daughters' tongues. So Clare just folded a warm, soft shawl over her arm but then she stepped into Rosie and Simon's car, taking care not to look at Simon's furious face as he watched this unprecedented mutiny.

It rained on the journey, drumming noisily on the roof as Rosie drove past Sellafield. The lads peered out through the rods of rain, excitedly searching for glowing cows or two headed sheep. Clare was staring anxiously at the back of Dan's seat as if battling with her thoughts.

"Dan, can I ask you something?"

Dan smiled. "Of course."

"How come you understand us women so well?"

Dan laughed. "Rosie might not agree with you there! But if you mean why do I take the women's side, it's because I've seen the inequality myself. As a teenager I was 'one of the lads', until I got friendly with a group of girls and watched the put downs, the sexual harassment and the bullying they endured. I was bullied myself for hanging round with girls. And the whole time the girls supported these jeering lads. It's been going on for generations, boys' privilege and power and girls' self sacrifice and oppression."

Clare nodded. "It makes you wonder if there's some kind of conspiracy."

"Well there is. It's called patriarchy." Dan replied. "We're all told we have differing roles, women being the nurturers, in the home. Men the leaders, out there running the world. And not doing a very good job of it neither. Wars, corrupt governments, racism, hatred, corporate criminality, hooliganism and of course, sexism. Simon and John are both examples of a belief in male superiority. Look how Simon sticks by John, with his dreadful behaviour and yet bullies you, even though you're the one who looks after him, his mother, his kids and the home."

Clare glanced out at the rain for a moment."You don't think it's me then?" she asked quietly.

Rosie snorted. "Of course it's not you. He's a bully. I saw it growing up with him. You should get a medal for putting up with him for so long. He's actually very insecure. Dan, can you get those biscuits out the bag?"while the kids were rustling she quietly continued. "Luckily his son has a gentle side I'm sure he's more like you. I don't think he'll follow in his footsteps."

"Yes, but what about Bethany?" In the silence Clare began to cry softly. She turned her head so the two boys playing on Niall's Tamagotchi behind her wouldn't notice.

"I don't know what to do?" Clare's face was anguished. Dan and Rosie glanced at each other and Dan swivelled round to take Clare's hand. "It's up to you of course but if you should decide to leave we'll support you."

"Rosie added "The lads get on so well."

Clare looked at her son. He had never looked so happy, engrossed in his game with Ewan. The spoilt and sullen boy seemed to have left. Hope drifted around her face as she stared out at fields, sheep, cows and farms being left behind as they whizzed past. Hot flashes of sun created sliding patterns inside the car roof, grey clouds moved above trees with glittering diamond canopies and Clare stirred. 'Yes, perhaps she could confide in Rosie, get help.'And this settled her.

The fuggy warmth, gentle motion and chill out music made them reluctant to get out of the car once they had swung into the castle car park but Ewan needed a wee. The grey floated away, leaving patches of blue sky, sudden white clouds and those moments of hot sun turning the canopy of these trees to a dancing, translucent gold. They decided not to wait for the others but left a message at the gate house then strolled down a drive with towering rhododendron bushes alongside. There was a fairy dell with tiny doors cut into the base of trees and wooden mushrooms to be used as tables in the clearings. Rows of fairy lights were slung through tree branches and tiny signs pointed to the castle attractions, the boys excitedly chasing each one, while pretending they were far too grown up and cool to be impressed by such childish frivolities. Celia teased them but couldn't disguise her own excitement. They heard the call of owls just as they read the sign 'Owl show here at 11 a.m.' So they followed the owl pictures alongside the wall, through an ivy draped gap to an outdoor enclosure, then sat on the half moon row of wooden benches and waited in anticipation. Two young women stepped through a gate, each carrying an owl on their arm. Celia squealed and leapt up from the bench, throwing her arms up in excitement. "Look at them. How cute are they?"

Both owls shook their feathers, displaying soft kaleidoscopes of muted greys, browns and creams, then swivelled their heads so that huge, unblinking eyes stared back at the family. On silent wings they swooped low over the entranced audience, deftly grabbed 'prey' from the fingers of a volunteer then glided with their reward to a perch. Meanwhile, another young woman brought two small wooden boxes and putting them on the ground, opened doors at the front. Immediately, a tiny, fluffy grey owlet rushed out of one of the boxes and headed straight over to a young girl's trainer to tug at the laces, causing the group of humans to mouth "Aahh" as one.

"It thinks it's a worm." Ewan whispered, eyes fixed on the bird.

"Do owls eat worms?" Rosie wondered, grabbing Celia's arm and tugging for her to sit down. Between the huge orange eyes and downy feathers fluffed round the claws, Rosie could understand Clare's urgent whisper "I so want to pick it up."

Suddenly, the other little owl came running out of its box and as if too shy to perform, hopped towards a man made burrow of sand and disappeared inside. The besotted fans all laughed and clapped as, after a few moments it came rushing out of the other end of the burrow. It started to rain but no one seemed to notice as an array of owls were brought out to fly, to dazzle, to entertain the damp humans. After the show, as the family headed for the tea rooms, they all agreed that though the large birds were glorious, it was the diminutive burrowing owls that won their hearts. Celia hoped the others would see the signs and go to the next show. Clare meanwhile, had realized that the path to the castle would be far too long for Grace to walk. So she asked one of the guides if he would get on his walkie talkie to the main gate and give a message to Simon to get a wheelchair for gran. She knew he would be indignant with her for telling him what to do. Nor would he want to take responsibility for his mother.She just hoped he wouldn't have a go at her in front of the others. She bent, seemingly to study a dazzle of azaleas over the wall. Tears slid down her face.

Simon pulled in the car park ahead of John just as the rain decided it really meant it.

"I'm going to stay here dad." Bethany exclaimed. "I haven't got a coat."

"Oh no you don't." Simon stated firmly. "If I've got to go through this, you're not getting out of it.

Bethany got out of the car, she knew better than to cross her dad.

The sports car pulled up alongside and John got out, then waited as from the back seat, Sapphire pushed her gran's backside to help Grace as she struggled out of the bucket seat. They congregated next to Rosie's car and Sapphire chirruped through the window to Celt who had recognized them and was whining, then turned back to the dejected group.

" Come on, let's get to the tea room." Simon led the way through the gate house. "Look at these admission prices, just to get a cup of tea."

"I'll pay Simon." Grace, short of breath, called, trying to catch up but still clinging to Sapphire.

"Come up here then mother. Pass me your purse."

Sapphire picked up a leaflet. "I'll pay for myself Gran." she insisted as she helped her gran to the desk. "But do you mind if I hurry ahead. There's an owl show? Do you want to come Bethany?"

"I am not going to get wet through watching a few birds fly over my head." Bethany snapped open an umbrella and slipped an arm through her dads.

Sapphire took the old lady's hand. " Uncle Simon will push you in a wheelchair, apparently it's a long way to the castle." She looked meaningfully at Simon then sprinted off.

"You don't need a wheelchair, do you mother?" It was a statement, not a question.

Grace wistfully eyed the wheelchairs in the corner, watched Sapphire's pink dreadlocks reflected on the glossy rhododendron leaves as she hurried away, then turned to Simon. "No dear, I'll be fine."

Rosie and entourage had crossed a courtyard and found the tea rooms in the old stable block where once horses had rested, but now each stall housed a pine table and sturdy benches. As she was ordering tea, Celia and the boys clamouring and pointing at their choice of cake the rest of the group arrived to add to the noise and confusion. Tables were lugged around, put together and cake orders were called, then changed. Sapphire plonked herself next to her dad.

"You wouldn't believe the way uncle John treated gran in the car" she whispered to him, "He kept the top down all the way and poor gran looked frozen. I kept telling him but he ignored me and we got rained on. Then she kept trying to talk to him, telling him how cute he was when he was a toddler. Do you know what he said to her? Will you stop wittering on mother? Well, her bottom lip started to wobble and she clammed up, so I told him off I'm afraid dad. There's a much worse way to have a pain in the butt than knackered springs." They smiled ruefully at one another. "Where is gran by the way?" Sapphire looked round the busy cafe.

Rosie stopped handing out cakes and stared at Simon. "Yes, where is mother?"

"She's sat on a bench about halfway up the drive." Simon plonked himself down and helped himself to a slice of coffee and walnut.

"Did you not get the message?" Dan asked.

Simon glared at Clare. "Yes."

"And you've just left her there, have you?" Rosie stood menacingly over him.

"She's alright" he said casually. "She told us to leave her, she'd just get her breath back."

"I told you she'd need a wheelchair, that drive's far too long for her." Clare spoke up angrily, then wondered at herself for not containing her temper.

"Sorry mum, I hurried ahead." Sapphire spoke up, "I'll nip back, grab a wheelchair, then rescue her, she'll be upset." And, with that, she leapt up and ran out the heavy stable doors.

"You could drink your tea." Rosie called, but she was gone.

"I may as well have that if it's going spare". John slid the cake and teacup across the table.

"I don't believe you two." Rosie glared at John then snarled at Simon but they were unconcerned.

Sat away from her family, Bethany was on her phone, dealing with her own mutinous crew. Jules was asking her if she still wanted the three tops she had got her from H and M.

“No, I don’t want them” Beth responded casually, “I got some tops from C and A.”

“Well, I’ve paid for them, I can’t take them back and they don’t fit me.” Jules started to sound annoyed.

“Look, I don’t want them. Sell ‘em to your mates, half your mates look like they could do with new clothes.” Bethany responded.

“So you’re not going to pay me then?”

“That’s what I said.”

“Don’t ask me to do you any favours anymore.”

“Oh fuck off. Stop making such a fuss.” and Bethany cut off the conversation.

Two elderly ladies in matching lilac cardigans and pleated skirts patted their perms and glanced at each other with raised eyebrows as they shuffled past.

“These new fangled phones you can carry round nowadays are just going to mean trouble.” the one assured. “People will just be able to row wherever they are.”

“Even in public. These youngsters nowadays.” the other agreed, nodding sagely.

Around the group there began another debate as to whether they should go round the rooms of the castle.

“If it’s raining we’ll look round inside. Right?” Rosie suggested.

“Fair enough” Ewan agreed, looking doubtful “But it’ll be boring.”

But struggling with the huge latches and going through each heavy oak door to find suits of armour standing guard in the medieval rooms slightly scared and thrilled the children. Creeping up the wide dark wood staircase with the eyes of ancestors staring down from ancient silver picture frames Celia came across grand velvet drapes inviting her to hide amongst their folds ready to ambush the lads.

Until, they reached a bedroom purported to be haunted by the ghost of Tom Foolery. The youngsters studied the murky photo of the strange figure in his diamond patterned suit.

"It feels really cold in here" Niall muttered after reading the story of the ghost who wandered through this very room.

"It's just your imagination." said Sapphire, looking carefully around the chamber.

"I'm going to wait and see if he appears," Ewan tried to sound matter of fact.

"Well I'm not standing here all day" Rosie retorted.

"Mum's scared" stated Celia but they all crowded behind Dan and Rosie as they stepped out of the room.

A swift shaft of sunlight sparked the mullioned windows till each pane looked as if it were on fire.

"The sun's shining. Let's go outside." Niall called.

"But there's the kitchens yet." Rosie's tone was hopeful.

"I'd have thought you'd seen enough of kitchens" Dan responded over his shoulder as there was a group exodus. She was left stood in an upstairs hallway. "Dan." she called as loudly as being in public would allow. His face poked back through the huge door.

"What?" quizzically.

Rosie moved to her side of the door, which was just as well as beside the window her hair framed her face in a flaming angry arc in the sun.

"You just went off. Never even considered what I said" she hissed.

"I was just following the kids." he countered.

"So it doesn't matter what I want?" She glanced round to check if other people were around. "Off you went."

"I guess I didn't want to lose them " Dan's voice was getting louder.

"Then why didn't you call them back?"

"Oh grow up Rosie."

Nearby people were studying fourteenth century vases and battle helmets too earnestly.

"Right. I will. I am going to look at grown up kitchen things like copper pots and pans. Things you won't be interested in." and Rosie pushed past her angry husband.

"I didn't say I wasn't interested. That's not fair." he called to her retreating back. "I do plenty of the cooking."

"More fool you." A pensioner, studying a huge painting of a knight astride black horse, muttered.

Dan glared then hurried after Rosie. He would like to have slammed the door but it was hard enough opening it up a few extra inches to allow himself to storm through.

Once they were all outside the air was sharp and clear as crystal, the sun a red glitter ball framed by thin, black clouds across an open sky. From the battlements the view looked as if it hadn't changed since the last invasion. The terraced gardens swept down beyond low stone walls to the sparkle of a river chasing alongside the thin ribbon of a road that buckled and curved, seemingly to the horizon. It was easy to imagine knights on horseback, holding pennants aloft and heading to the hills to battle an army of knights with pennants and shields of a different colour and crest.

Suddenly Celia took off running down the first steep embankment, whooping loudly.

"Joie de Vivre" Dan said, smiling. "It's too steep." yelled Clare.

"Why does she do these things?" Bethany glanced up from her phone.

And immediately, Celia was flat on her back and sliding at a good pace across the grass towards the first wall.

"Oh no" Rosie groaned.

Somehow Celia had managed to turn her body and was heading in a different direction. There was a huge rustle, a bird squawked in alarm and shot into the air above a moving rhododendron bush. Then Celia appeared from a hole amongst the branches and leaves and limped back up the hill.

"Not again" Rosie cried.

"Your daughter certainly likes to get messy." Grace announced in disdain.

"Are you hurt?" Clare called but Celia just grinned and stuck up her thumb.

"Look at that bush." Rosie nodded towards the damaged evergreen. She then gazed at Dan, they kissed and interlocked fingers, both mumbling 'Sorry.'

"On that note I think we'd better leave the scene of the crime and head on back to the cottage." Dan suggested as Celia staggered past.

"Look at her back," said Ewan.

Everyone exploded with laughter at the sight of Celia's jacket, trousers and even hair. There was one huge streak of grey sloppy mud from the top of her head to her boots.

"Where did Simon and John go?" Clare looked around.

"There's a small cellar at the back of the castle that hosts a bar" Sapphire said, "I think we'll find them in there."

"Two of the drivers." Rosie was annoyed. "Clare, are you ok to drive your car?"

Clare looked agitated. "Simon doesn't like me driving his car."

"Too bad. Grace and Sapphy will have to go in with you and John will have to take his chances with me driving his car."

So, with Celia leading the way, walking like a scarecrow, liquid dripping off her sleeves and fingers, the families headed towards the car park, just stopping at the bar en route to collect the two drinkers. There was another exchange at the cars. Simon insisted on driving but Rosie was mad and in no uncertain terms told him he was over the limit, literally pushed him into the tiny seat in the back of John's tiny sports car, plonked herself behind the wheel and indicated to John to clamber into the passenger seat. He didn't even object, he knew he was over the limit. Simon started yelling to Clare to swap places with John but Rosie slammed her door and roared off, spraying up gravel as she spun out of the car park. Clare got a glimpse of Simon's contorted face through the narrow back window as Niall grabbed her hand.

"Come on mum, we need you to drive the Audi."

"Can we come with you?" Celia raced to the immaculate white car and threw herself onto the back seat. "Come on Gran, you're up front."

"I hope I'm not driving." Grace laughed. "It's a good job you've took your coat off as well, young lady." She nodded at the pristine seats but there was a new sparkle in her eyes and she patted Celia's shoulder affectionately.

"Wait for me." Ewan leapt in next to Celia.

Dan rolled down his window. "Don't worry about me, Billy no mates driving home on his own."

"What you moaning about, you've got the dog?" Ewan yelled from the open window of the Audi but the wind swept away his words into the trees. The old Ford chugged past as Dan attempted to race them out of the car park.

Later, back at Cloud cottage the sun moved across from the window, so that Rosie and Dan, chatting amiably in the warm steamy kitchen, found themselves suddenly chopping vegetables and stuffing a pork joint in the gloom. Rosie pretended not to see Dan's hands cutting carrots beside her, acting as if her knife was slipping towards his fingers. He flicked a tea towel at the back of her legs, then laughing, they started to run around the kitchen until they both crashed into an open cupboard door, sliding to the floor in a hug which led easily into a breathtaking giant snog. Inevitably, the door flew open and three noisy young people chased each other into the kitchen. Niall, in front, slid to a stop, his mouth dropped open and eyes widened. Ewan, more used to his parents, started tutting loudly.

"They're at it again."

Celia hissed in mock disgust.

"Haven't you got anything better to do than spoil our fun?" Dan pulled away from the smirking Rosie. "Go and bother somebody else. We're busy getting dinner ready."

"So I see" said Ewan.

Niall looked embarrassed, he wasn't used to displays of affection between adults.

"I've just had an idea. Come on." Celia turned round and shot out of the kitchen.

"Celia, what are you up to?" Rosie called but the doorway was empty.

"Oh well, let's get on with our vegetables" Dan suggested, his eyes twinkling as he helped Rosie get off the floor and into his arms once more.

The sun was sending golden shafts of warm light across the lounge illuminating Celia and the lads standing silently behind John's armchair. He was holding the Daily Mirror in front of his face but the loud snores assured them he was fast asleep. Celia took a lipstick out of a make up bag and handed it to Niall. They were up to mischief again.

"Where did you get this from?" he mouthed.

"It's Bethany's" she responded, silently passing a black kohl pencil to Ewan.

Gently Niall painted a pair of bright red lips on John's bald spot.

"She'll kill you if she finds out" he whispered.

Ewan drew a pair of eyes above the lips and the hair on top of John's head formed a perfect fringe. They all started giggling "And he'll kill us all if he wakes up" Celia added.

The trio fought hard to control themselves as Celia clipped the 'fringe' away from the eyes with two pink hair clips. Then they all fled to the sanctuary of the shed where they could let their laughter explode.

John slept on and now his head had dropped down showing a strange female face on a man's body, the lips glowing brightly in the sun. To try and make up for turning Uncle John into a painted doll {though she thought it was well worth it} Celia set the table for dinner with help from Ewan and even Niall. They had done an amazing job, crimson azaleas and chrysanthemums from the garden in glass bowls on a white embroidered tablecloth. They had even cut out animal shapes and coloured them as place settings. Clare was an elegant giraffe, the neck gently curved but sadness in the eyes beneath the long, luxurious lashes. Rosie was a smiling, satisfied cat and Dan, of course, a large sturdy horse with mischief on its face. Grace was a silver Koi carp with shimmering, trailing fins and tail to represent her outfits. Although, they had made Simon a hyena, (Niall made that one) and Celia had made a walrus with tusks and a face that was an amazing likeness to Uncle John's. So that her mother would completely forgive them, Celia had walked down the hill into Keswick for Bramley apples and fresh raspberries to make a pie for pudding.

When everyone came down from napping or reading in their rooms they all sat down in their usual places without comment. Except Clare.

"Oh Celia, this looks beautiful" she exclaimed.

And when she heard that Niall had been involved she was delighted.

"Niall, I didn't realize you were so artistic. These place settings look amazing. I need my glasses to see what the animals are. I'll just fetch them."

Niall preferred his mum not to see what animal he had chosen for his dad. "Don't bother mum" he said. But he beamed.

When John bent down to pick up his napkin both Dan and Rosie, sitting opposite, spotted the art work on his head. They both gasped then looked to Celia, who was busying herself by helping Grace get seated. They then looked towards Clare who was pretending to blow her nose on her napkin.

"Don't do that dear" said Grace, who then wondered why a mild reprimand could be so funny. This attracted the attention of Simon who spotted the face as John, unawares ,was shovelling prawn cocktail into the lower mouth.

Simon was not amused. “You should tell him Clare.”

“You tell him” she retorted uncharacteristically.

“Tell who what?” Grace asked, which set them off into paroxysms again.

But no-one told John and later Simon punished the culprits by making them wash all the pots by hand. Again, Celia thought it was well worth it.

Looking round the table, Simon decided that everyone was getting too cosy, having too much fun, so picking up the bottles of wine, he began his Rosie campaign.

“Red or white Rosie?” he asked, pouring her wine .“Now, do you want to tell us about this job of yours?

Rosie looked pleasantly surprised at this unusual interest. She talked about how she loved her job as a women’s refuge worker. How it involved drama and adventure, her roles ranging from counsellor to caretaker, fund raiser to child therapist. It was stimulating, sometimes heart breaking and she needed to keep her wits about her. She glanced around the table to make sure everyone was interested and was reassured to see that all eyes were on her. So she recalled the times when she rang the police to get a perpetrator removed from where he was lurking down the street or when a woman had to leave for sneaking a man into her room. There were occasions when she escorted a woman back to her home to fetch her belongings only to find them ripped up and strewn around the rooms, then would give comfort and counsel. She had to be an emergency plumber when at nine o clock on a Sunday night an ancient pipe burst and as there was never enough money she had to come up with ingenuous schemes to fund the project. Dan nodded in agreement as she recalled the sleepless nights as inspiration eluded her, until she thought of asking the women themselves and discovered how creative bored women could be. She smiled as she recalled the Chef of the Year award for the younger teenagers in the refuge. That produced some amazing meals for the residents and gave one young girl the opportunity to serve up her rack of lamb with apricot and pistachio rubble on a bed of braised fennel for a cookery contest on television.

Rosie's audience laughed as she imitated one of the mother's in a perfect Liverpool accent. "Our Kirsty's never shown any interest in cooking before."the gobsmacked mother had informed the local newspaper. But then there was the dilemma of how to conceal the whereabouts of the refuge and its new celebrity while encouraging the young girl's talents. The other mothers turned to their own protege wondering what accomplishments may be concealed beneath their uncooperative exteriors. There were story and poetry writing competitions which disclosed some dark events in the children's lives. This, the counsellors assured the alarmed mothers, would aid their healing."

"That sounds amazing, all that you're doing." Clare enthused. "From misery comes talent."

Simon glared at his wife. " So why aren't the wives and mothers sorting this out themselves instead of it coming out of our taxes?" Now he wished he'd never asked about the job. "O.K. Rosie, you're doing a good job but let's face it, is it worth all the expense for just a few women."

"You what. It's a massive problem. It does happen to a few men as well but we're talking far more women, 1 in 4 in fact."

Simon grimaced, "Have you ever heard the expression lies, more lies and damned statistics?"

"But these statistics are true Simon" Rosie said grimly.

"Oh come on, women have got it all nowadays. I don't even know what you're talking about." he said with a twisted smile.

"Where do I begin? Because of our patriarchal world, men have been fed the idea that they are superior to women, they have the right to be boss, in charge of the relationship, in charge of the world."

"Now where on earth would men get the impression that they have the right to boss women around?"

Rosie realized she was being wound up and decided to give her brother a run for his money. "That's rich, coming from you. But let's go back in history to the Bible. Our societies were formed on God's words were they not?."

"I thought you didn't believe in God"

"I don't, but a lot of people do. Please note that nearly every religious leader is a man and the old testament especially is littered with instructions on controlling women. "

"Rubbish. As a Christian I deeply resent what you are saying. What about Mary, mother of Jesus, she's an important figurehead."

"Hah, She couldn't even have sex. She had to be a virgin. A vessel for the important cargo."

"Rosie, please. The children." Grace called but the speaker was too incensed to hear.

" If those male scribes who wrote the whole bloody bunch of myths thought they could get away with it, Jesus would have come out of God's navel or the top of his head."

Simon was trying to keep his calm. "It's the Bible that instructs men to protect women because they are weaker. Of course it's right for men to be in charge. Adam was made in God's image. Eve came from Adam to be his helpmate, his comfort."

There are many places in the Bible that suggest male chastisement of women." Rosie countered. "And many men are far from our protectors. If they were I wouldn't be doing the job I am doing."

"We do not control women." Simon tried to firmly shut down the conversation.

"So why is it only the bride who says 'Obey' at a wedding service? Why is it her father 'Gives her away?'

Rosie had stood up and was leaning across the table.

Sapphire glanced across at the boys in alarm.

"I don't really think Simon wants to hear your opinions on religion Rosie." Grace, shocked, interrupted her "And you shouldn't be swearing like that in front of the children."

"Sorry mum but this is important stuff." Rosie didn't look sorry, just angry.

This conversation was not going the way Simon had expected. He thought he would wind his sister up but he was the one getting hot under the collar, while everyone at the table was silent and watching.

"And while we're talking history" Rosie continued calmly now "What do you think the persecution of witches in medieval times was all about?"

Simon laughed. He was back on safe ground. To be insulting about something he felt strongly about, his faith, was one thing but no one liked witches. "A bunch of old hags who deserved everything they got."

"Hah! You didn't realize then, those old hags were respected midwives, healers, counsellors and wise women of the villages and a threat to the new religion from Rome. They had to be disgraced so that people would turn from Paganism to Catholicism. They were set up, Pagans had no devil for the witches to consort with, the familiars were just pets, marks of the devil were birthmarks or moles, riding broomsticks and cooking babies were just cruel lies." She paused for breath, Simon had turned puce.

"You go mum" Sapphire called across the table.

"Please can you two stop it" Grace pleaded "It's so upsetting."

"A load of codswallop, blasphemous codswallop." was all Simon could say in response and John glanced up from his dinner to nod in agreement.

Clare was listening intently. She knew she was one of the 1 in 4, she was learning that it was happening to other women and where these male beliefs of superiority originated. She felt a deep intense anger coming up through her stomach. All these years she had put up with the sarcasm, the gaslighting, the nasty snipes. She had believed him when Simon had said it was her fault, or her imagination or her behaviour. The shame was not hers to carry round, it was his. She continued to sit quietly and observe the drama unfolding at the table. Niall and Ewan had stopped their game of sliding their greens over to one another's plates and were also listening. The dog skulked off as voices raised and Celia had stopped passing cauliflower cheese to her under the table. Even Bethany was only pretending to look at her phone as she listened to her father and aunt.

Simon drew himself up and lowered his voice menacingly.

"Like all these feminists Rosie, you're hard. You don't think women should be gentle, quiet creatures to balance men's forceful natures. No, really you feminists envy men. You want to be like us and that's why you're so strident. You know what, I'm sick of men, particularly white European men, getting the blame for all the ails of the world, from the environment to women's depression."

"It's not without cause though, is it?" Her voice rising again. " What gender are most prisoners? If a woman is walking down the street late at night would it be a group of men or women coming towards her that would make her nervous? Who were and still are, the slave masters and traders? What sex are the ruthless, cheating business men, there's a clue for you, we hear about? Who mainly abuses children? If you hear a thief creeping up the stairs do you expect it to be a man or woman's face poking round the bedroom door? The same if we hear of someone abusing their partner or children. Are you getting the picture Simon? And then we say 'Why does she put up with it? But shouldn't we be asking 'Why does he do it?' It's everywhere, in every society. Where do women go? Who believes them? Who respects them? Who acknowledges their fears?"

"Erm mum." Celia ventured but Rosie was too incensed to hear.

"Well I don't respect you when you get on your high horse like this. There's plenty of nasty women and I'm beginning to think you're one of them." Simon retaliated. He could feel the sand shifting under his feet. "Hang on. You get plenty of nasty women bosses. I've seen it myself. Women managers telling tales on their female staff to male bosses or favouring men workers."

"I do want you to understand that it's been thousands of years of conditioning on both sexes that's created these separate roles and I'm not unsympathetic to men's plight too but what about Wars, Simon?"

"Yes. And where would your women be if the men didn't go out risking their lives to protect them?" Simon sat back triumphantly.

"But who starts the Wars? And for what? Not to protect women. We become victims of your Wars – raped and killed. No, it's for money, for land, for resources and mainly for power. Look at all the dictators we've had through the ages and still have. Look at Genghis Kahn, Hitler, Polpot, Idi Amin. Look at European Imperialism. It made the misery of millions just the unfortunate collateral damage of enterprise. Do you want more?" Rosie paused and looked round her mesmerized audience but didn't give anyone a chance to respond.

"And here's another thing. What about all the women trying to bring up children with no fathers because they've walked out? Often for another woman. Or they say they can't cope with noisy kids. Or they use the excuse that she nags. Well women nag Simon when men don't listen."

"We're having no choice but to listen now, are we?" Simon spoke up.

" I haven't even started on the unequal treatment at work, or the War on nature. Or how some men don't think they should 'babysit' their own kids. Hah. Or clean the toilet. Or don't let women speak up at meetings or boardrooms or school."

"Right on. You go mum." Sapphire called.

Dan tapped Rosie's arm hesitantly. "I thought we said when we got here we'd keep our traps shut."

Simon had stood up and was glaring at Rosie face to face across the table. "You're talking out your arse."

There was a general gasp. Clare was beginning to grasp the big picture and squeezed Rosie's hand in solidarity, Simon noted this betrayal.

All eyes turned to Rosie who stared calmly back.

"That's just the response I would have expected from you."

Grace glanced at the faces around the table. 'If only Rosie didn't rock the boat.' She recalled times when, as a child Simon had calmly refused to do as she had asked and argued with her. Yet when she turned to his father for reinforcement he had laughed and told her to leave the boy alone. The times when she had talked to him about John's behaviour, tying up the dog at the back of the shed, tormenting next door's two girls, refusing to tell her where he had been when he was supposed to be at school, Harry had just responded with 'Boys will be boys' or gone completely over the top and took his belt off. How ineffectual she had felt, how unhappy these times in their childhood had made her. And then came along this brave, exuberant girl who would fearlessly support her mother and challenge her brothers, often getting herself into trouble with her stern father who had no qualms about punishing his daughter, trying to break her spirit. It had made Grace both fearful for her and ashamed of herself. Now, this family were helping her see that it was not her fault.'

Sapphire broke Grace's reverie when she came to rescue the situation.

“Come on everybody. The kids went to a lot of trouble to get this table looking so nice, the least we can do is eat. It looks like Uncle John is going to scoff all the pork on his own.”

The spell was broken. They all looked at John who was calmly chewing his way through a massive piece of meat and they all laughed, except Simon, who sat down again, a look of fury on his face.

“This looks delicious, well done Dan and Rosie.” said Clare and the audience clapped, whether it was for preparing the dinner or in support of Rosie’s rant was not clear. The meal carried on without issue. John steadily worked his way through two bottles of expensive Sauvignon, while Simon watched his progress with annoyance. His brother had left him out on a limb. The youngsters chatted amongst themselves, Bethany was unresponsive when asked her opinion on Rosie’s views, picking at her dinner and constantly checking her phone. Grace talked about the short career she loved with the local government during the War and how she went back to being a housewife at a time when there was food rationing and no money for infrastructure, schools or wages. Clare was not listening, she was thinking about what Rosie had said and things were starting to click into place, both in her own life and society as a whole. She had been trying to survive by placating a man who saw himself as her superior. She realized she could never please him and thought ‘Why should she because it wasn’t her problem but his?’ This realization made her choke on a carrot and all the wasted years and she sobbed out loud. Rosie looked over, together they got up from the table and arm in arm they left the room.

“I guess we’ll have pudding later, should we?” Celia called plaintively.

“We could still have ours.” Ewan stated. It was an interesting exchange but not enough to warrant going without pudding.

Sapphire glanced across at Grace who had stopped her reminiscing and was sadly staring at her hands twisting a handkerchief in her lap. She glanced meaningfully towards Celia who understood the silent message.

"Gran, tell me how you managed to bring up three children and teach piano from home with very little help?" Celia asked, moving into the seat next to her grandmother and taking hold of the agitated hand. Grace immediately brightened and took her mind back to happier times when her boys were adorable even though they were 'naughty' and she was young, strong and vigorous, sustained by a few good friends and a loving, supportive daughter.

Simon waited for someone to serve his pudding, while John, more used to fending for himself but unused to such tasty home made meals, cut a huge piece of apple and raspberry pie, pouring half a jug of cream on top. Dan retired to his room, full from the heavy meal, leaving the cleaning up in the hope that John might take the hint and do his fair share. John merely moved to the settee, flopped back and lit a cigar. Simon hurried up to his room as soon as he had instructed the kids on the washing up. He was concerned about the influence his dreadful sister was having on his impressionable wife. She was up there with her now, filling her head with more of the rubbish she had spouted over dinner. He stormed into the bedroom, ready to send his sister out with a flea in her ear but the only voices came from the television, the room was empty. He could hear an earnest conversation coming through the wall from the bedroom next door, There was some sobbing and over that, Dan was explaining something. Simon was outnumbered, how could he possibly go into their room and demand his wife come back in with him? What if she refused? Deflated and furious, he plonked himself on the bed and tried to engross himself with the thriller on the screen but found himself constantly trying to listen through the wall.

In the next bedroom Dan was squashed into a pink nursing chair. He was trying to look casual so as not to alarm Clare but his bum barely fitted into a 1920's seat designed for a woman and he had to lean forward as if intent on her every word.

I'd have thought his sister would have been the last person I could confide in." Clare was saying. "The trouble is I feel like he can hear me even when he's not around." Her voice lowered.

"That's because he's in there." Rosie tapped her head. "He can't really hear you."

She dismissed the troubling thought that maybe Simon could hear through the wall. She definitely heard his heavy plod coming up the stairs but reassured herself that even the inside walls were about a metre thick. And yes, the walls were doing their job, the ear pressed against the other side could only hear the voices as if under water, a muffled mix of a low pitch, higher sharps and fluid whimpers. Infuriatingly!

Reassured, Clare carried on. "He takes everything I do for granted., never acknowledges my efforts. He wouldn't do anything around the house, you know, like you emptied the dishwasher and cooked some of the meals Dan." Clare's voice trailed off and a look of guilt crept up her face.

"He sees anything in the kitchen as women's work and beneath him." Dan responded.

"Yet he expects us to see him as the master of the household when he's hardly ever there." Clare spoke bitterly now."When he does honour us with his presence he trots off to his office to do 'paperwork'.

"That means reading the paper or taking a nap." Rosie sniggered.

Clare continued without laughing. "I don't know myself anymore. I feel without purpose or use and I couldn't make a decision if it reached up and bit me on the bum. I know it sounds impossible but I always used to be such a positive person. I know I'm being disloyal but I'm at the end of my tether to be honest. And it's affecting the kids." A sob escaped. She turned the chair so she was unable to see her reflection in the dressing table mirror.

"So is this holiday a bit of a last chance saloon?" Rosie was serious now.

"Yes, but I don't know if I've got the guts to go. He runs the household budget, I have no money of my own and he would be more furious at paying out a settlement than me leaving him. Then I have to consider the kids. What about their schooling, their friends? Not that either of them seem to have many friends." Clare suddenly looked up to stare at Rosie, sat on the bed, supported by pillows. "I bet you wonder why I married him? What a fool eh?"

"Not at all." Rosie reached to take her hand. "Don't forget I grew up with him. I bet Mr Prince Charming assured you he'd never met anyone like you before when you met."

"Yes. You do know him well."

"You see it all with my job. I just wish I'd been there for you, I should have known better. Keeping away was the worst thing I could do."

"You tried very hard. I just felt so ashamed. And, of course, what he said went. He got me to make the excuses." Clare stopped suddenly, hung her head. "Oh, I shouldn't be saying all this, you've come here for a holiday." "We're here to help if we can." Dan said quietly.

So Clare continued. He's never been violent, that's one thing. He knew I would have left then. But he puts me right on every idea or point of view I had. Out would come all the reasons he was right and I was wrong. I often tried to sit him down to have a discussion but the whole conversation would be dismantled and twisted until I either gave up or agreed. He can confound me with a look, confuse me with an argument, scare me by raising his voice or banging doors, often in front of the kids."

"What about your friends?" Rosie asked.

"I didn't see my work colleagues after I left nursing. They were my friends. I agreed to look after Grace so I have been stuck in the house ever since. Our only other friends were couples I met through Simon and their relationships seemed a lot like ours."

At 2.30 Simon gave up trying to decipher the buzzing on the other side of the wall. His ear was hot and sore and he could no longer concentrate or keep his eyes open. He banged around cleaning his teeth and opening cupboard doors but finally crept into bed, face set into stern features and immediately fell asleep.

"His wife did not come back into the room until the early hours when she settled on the chaise longue with a pillow and blanket.

Tuesday

Plans and Pleasures

Dan had escaped the icy atmosphere that seemed to hover over the dining table and linger around the empty sofa in the lounge from the altercations the night before. The sharp chill of autumn had blown the bedroom curtains and woke him up, so that carefully he slid out of bed so as not to wake Rosie. Now, standing in the middle of the lawn, he looked up at the rows of windows, the curtains concealing the sleeping people within. There was a fine ground mist and the lawn sparkled and squeaked beneath his boots, leaving ethereal footprints in his wake. A soggy blackbird swooped past him then rose up chattering its alarm. Two thrushes were running fast across the grass, then stopping suddenly, heads on one side listening for worms. A watery sun peered between the trees, unable yet to provide any warmth below.

Dan headed for a stand of trees just beyond the garden and stopped to admire the jagged patterns of bark that made up the cream and grey stripes of a silver birch. His hands touched the rough textures and his mind's eye pictured a pub bar fronted by these glorious trunks and topped with gleaming copper beer pumps. His vision began to take shape as he stared around the copse. A pub in the middle of the city, a cabin completely made of wood with dark oak panelling within, illuminated by crystal chandeliers, scattered pine chairs and tables with just one wall built of old bricks housing a huge fireplace. 'Insurance could be a bit steep' he considered fleetingly. And real trees. In old beer barrels, perhaps with white fairy lights in their branches. Ivy growing around the doorways and up entwined around the beams, that lovely, glossy green sheen against the dark of the wood. He would bring wildness and nature into the city centre. Surely that was what people craved, was missing from their lives? The sacred, the free, the ancient could uplift spirits and soothe troubled souls more effectively than the spirits in their glass? He considered how lost some men were, many looking for something to believe in, to replace their absent, uncaring or cruel fathers. He would hold seminars in this natural oasis, get guys to talk and teach them how to release their egos from the need to control, to learn to trust and show their feelings.

'I'll call it 'Bar Free'. That'll get them in' he mused and was amazed at how abruptly this powerful idea had come into his head. Like it had been sitting there waiting for the right moment to make an entrance.

He began to feel excited about this idea. It would combine enjoyment with learning. It would be a social enterprise, he would get funding and call it 'Bar Free at The Public House Academy'. Like old time pubs where men and women were ushered into separate bars. 'No actually,' he thought, 'women were discouraged from going into pubs at all.' There would be classes for women too on self esteem and confidence. In a separate bar women would feel free to speak up without being made fun of. Perhaps Rosie would run that side of things, raising awareness of inequality, it would be right up her street and she would be good at it too.

Dan had been purposefully walking across the lawn to the trees and back again in a non stop circle, talking to himself and waving his arms while he conceived his plan. One small figure was spying on this performance through the bedroom curtains and chuckling to himself. Ewan grabbed his dressing gown and ran outside, gasping at the chill in the air and under his bare feet, to prance across the lawn to the trees, round and round, laughing with his dad.

"I'm so glad you're my dad," he glanced up at the kindly face, "Even though you talk to yourself."

"And I'm glad you're my son. Even though you'll soon be taller than me and I will really, really resent you."

"Niall tells me stuff about his dad. I feel sorry for him." Ewan slipped his hand into Dan's.

"Between you and me, Simon's an idiot. I'm glad you've befriended Niall."

"Yeh. It all kicked off last night, didn't it?" Ewan said.

"Only a few more days to go and we can go home, away from Rosie's crazy family." said Dan.

"I like it here though, there's something about this place. I'm having a good time dad. And I think Niall is too."

Dan nodded in agreement."Yeh but I feel sorry for your mother. She deserves a decent family."

"She's got us." Ewan said.

"And she's got uncle John" responded his dad. And they both stop, glance at each other and giggle, then carry on their circuit.

"I feel sorry for auntie Clare as well." said Ewan.

Suddenly the gate creaked and rattled and Sapphire in bright green pyjamas ran towards them.

"What's going on here then?" Sapphire asked, falling in with their steps.

"For goodness sake, can't a man cook up a brilliant and wealth creating plan without the rest of the family wanting to get in on the act?" Dan put on a stern face. "Oh, here comes another one now."

Celia was skipping barefoot across the wet grass, her hair flying behind her, a coat flung across her pyjamas. She diverted to kick a pyramid of mouldering leaves by the shrubbery then ran to grab her dad's arm.

"Alright, what's going off?" she insisted.

"Dad's got a brilliant plan he's going to tell us all about." Sapphire did two cartwheels then stopped in front of Dan.

As the merry band continued their circuit below, a forlorn face watched from a casement window.

'If only her family were happy like that.' For the first time since their marriage, Clare had not rushed to make her husband a cup of tea that morning. She knew Simon would recognize this small gesture as a symbolic act of defiance and had no idea how he would react. But she knew it would mean trouble. Just as the sleepless night she had spent on the chaise longue in their bedroom portrayed more than angry words could ever do. She dreaded the backlash but felt sustained by her new knowledge. For Clare knew her attitudes had changed, things were just not going to be the same, no matter what Simon said or did. And this difference was because of her new understanding and the support she felt around her in this house. Sadly, she reflected on the charming man she first met. The man who hung on to her every word, who seemed to like all her friends, who surprised her with tickets when Clannad, her favourite group, were on tour, who seemed to adore her. Why had he turned into this tyrant? Where did her soulmate go? Did she have such poor judgment? Sat at the dressing table, brooding into the mirror, a resolution was beginning to take shape.

She knew that she was miserable and confused, that she had to take care what she said around Simon, that she was in the habit of placating him but also sensed she was the gatekeeper between the kids and their father, that if she stepped out of line they might suffer his wrath. She was continually shocked, searching for the considerate man she married in his tone of voice and behaviour. Sometimes, when he thought she might disclose to friends or even leave, he became that caring man again. Now she had left her job to look after Grace she had no income of her own, which made her feel even more dependent. Her thoughts tossed around, one minute she was sure she had the strength to just walk away to a new life, the next she wondered how Simon would cope with his mother and possibly Bethany. It broke her heart to think that Bethany might choose to stay with her father and the decision might be on something as tenuous as not wanting to leave their posh house. Clare hoped she would get some time alone with Rosie again to talk it all through. She could feel her resolve sliding. His stern voice was back in her head. She was so tired.

And suddenly he was back in the room looking unkempt and tired. He strode across to stand behind her and regard her reflection.

“What’s up with you? Aren’t you having a good time?”

Clare forced herself to address him through the mirror and speak firmly through trembling lips. “Simon. I’m not happy. It’s our relationship that’s doing it.” She paused. “ I’m seriously thinking of leaving you.”

His hand on her shoulder tightened. Clare pushed away, leapt up and rushed out of the room before he could say anything. ‘There I’ve said it.’ she thought and relief rushed as she hurried down the stairs to look for someone, anyone to be with.

There was a tacit agreement between the families that this was going to be an indoor day of rest after their busy trips. It was a blustery wet day, a sky the colour of dirty linen. Soft yellow lamps and a glowing log fire created a soothing palette against the constant hum and tap of the wind and rain that rattled the windows. Even Celia and the boys were quiet, busy with their own pastimes. Celia had been collecting autumn wild flowers, leaves and fir twigs to put, together with favourite poems and photographs, in her scrapbook. She enjoyed this craft, the cover had been diligently constructed with glued green wool tartan and each page of her collections represented all the things she loved most, nature, her family and thought provoking or inspiring literature. Every so often she glanced up at her mum on the sofa, from her position stretched out on the rug. She noticed, at times the paper would shudder, then fall and Celia would get a glimpse of her mum's face. Behind the curtain of swinging hair, her eyes were shut and mouth open. Then the paper would get abruptly lifted up and Rosie would glare at the grinning onlooker before resuming her nap. It had been a long, sleepless night.

Dan worked in the kitchen, papers for his project spread out all across the units. Sometimes he would start tutting as one of his drawings got stuck in a dob of marmalade or jam then would rip when he tried to lift the sheet off. He began to feel a draught round his legs and on investigation, found the conservatory door wide open from when John had left to wander down to the pub, smudgy mixes of colour still discernible on his bald patch. Sapphire was on the window seat, strumming her latest composition on her guitar. Inspiration seemed to be effortless in this room. Dan tutted again, loudly this time.

“Can't you feel that draught Sapphire? No, not draught. It's a gale. We don't live in a barn you know.”

“Sorry dad.” Sapphire clambered out of her creative reverie. “I didn't notice.”

“Well your bloomin' hands are blue, look at 'em.”

She glanced absentmindedly at her hands, then carried on strumming and gently singing.

"I'll shut this door then, should I?" Dan purposefully shut and locked the glass door, the sarcasm lost on his daughter.

Back in the kitchen, many of his papers had blown down onto the flagstones and some looked decidedly damp.

'Is this an omen? Should I not go ahead with this programme?' he thought grimly as he blew on each sheet before putting them back on the counter.

Just then Simon strolled in, heading for the biscuit tin. Dan glanced up, then back to the mess of papers and inspiration lit up his face. He smiled up at Simon.

"You know a lot about setting up your own business don't you?"

"I should think so. I've started up three over the years."

"Could I ask a bit of advice then?"

Simon looked surprised, even flattered. "Go ahead."

"What do I need to start a social enterprise? I've got the practical side really clear in my mind but what else do I need to figure out?"

"Costs." Simon scoffed. "And profits."

"Of course, I'd not really thought of them."

Simon rolled his eyes. "You're not going to be in business very long then. What is it you're setting up?"

"A city centre bar. I've always wanted to run a bar but not just any old bar. I want to use my background as a social worker to help men. I thought I'd have a side room and advertise, put up signs inviting anyone who might want to come along to the Might Club."

"What the hell's the Might Club?"

“It’s a peaceful Fight Club. You must have seen the film. But here the pen is mightier than the sword, so to speak. Men will be able to talk, discuss their problems and hopefully their feelings. I hope to explain how damaging it is to believe you have to be tough, powerful, unreachable.” Dan glared defensively at the top of Simon’s head as he was dividing a paper into columns.

“Sounds bollocks. You’re as nutty as your wife. Putting that aside,- you should be thinking about how you’re going to make it profitable. Here, look, there’s no time to get this onto your laptop so I’m doing a graph.Costs, location, rent or buy, loans, overheads.” Writing in the columns Simon now felt in familiar territory. Discussing start-ups excited him. “First and foremost how much cash have you got to work with?” He glanced expectantly at Dan.

“I’m going to sell a barn to finance it.”

“O.K. I know a guy I can put you in touch with for that. Next. Location. This is where many entrepreneurs come unstuck. Location is massively important.”

“I’m going to build a cabin in the centre of the city so I need a plot”

“You’ve lost the plot. And I can’t help you with that. You’ll have to find it yourself. I suppose you don’t know what city?”

“Not yet.”

“I can point you in the direction of a good company that sells and delivers wooden cabins to put en-situ. I can’t believe I’m even going along with this.”

The two men grinned. “You know I would normally be charging a huge fee for this don’t you?”

Simon pulled up a stool to the counter and the two heads touched as they pored over the spread sheet.

Meanwhile, the boys were absorbed in building a Lego Star Wars system in their bedroom. The only sound was the rattle of the pieces as their hands scuttled through them like spiders, looking for tiny pieces of spaceship.

Grace was having a lie-in with the pretence that she needed to sort her wardrobe out, a good excuse now that she had been browbeaten into going to Sapphire's concert. There was a cup of cold tea and the dish with her dentures still soaking on the bedside table. Rosie had crept in to see if she wanted to come down for the late breakfast and crept out again to announce that mum was still asleep so had left her.

Despite the annoyances of the family, especially Rosie, Simon later found himself secretly enjoying the sophomoric effects of the house. He had lain in the bath for an hour, only moving to turn on the hot tap with his toe, the Daily Mirror a damp, crumpled mess on the floor. He hadn't had a bath for years, didn't have time, only allowing himself a hurried daily shower. For a little while all was peaceful in Simon's world as he allowed himself to drift off thinking of Clare, how annoying she was being but not for one moment, life without her. It was strange how tranquil the house was. The gurgle of radiators, the dripping of the old taps, the bustling wind and rain at the old stained glass window, normally irritating sounds here had a calming effect.

It was late afternoon, Rosie put down her Guardian as Niall raced into the lounge with Ewan close behind. In seeing his aunt stretched out he slid to a stop and Ewan crashed into his back, causing him to fall flat on his face across the footstool and Rosie's legs. He was chagrined, a new look for Niall.

"I'm so sorry Auntie." he mumbled, glaring at Ewan.

"I saw what happened there, don't worry. I'm glad you've come in actually. I wanted to ask what you thought of George Monbiot?" Rosie tapped a picture and article in the broadsheet.

"Oh, he's a troublemaker, he is. A Scaremonger filling everyone's heads with rubbish."

He was so assured. Rosie knew where this had come from.

"I think he's amazing." Ewan added. Niall stared at him in disbelief. Just then Simon strolled in.

"Simon. We were just talking about George Monbiot"

"Here we go" Ewan said flatly.

"He's a trouble maker he is. Trying to get everyone to believe the world is coming to an end." Simon's tone was vicious.

"Told you" Niall looked at Ewan.

"Let's get out of here before they start." Ewan shoved his cousin across the room and through the french windows to face a sudden gusty squall of rain. An argument began behind them as they left, voices raised and travelled up to the rest of the family upstairs.

Clare was back in the bedroom, leaning out of her window, watching a herd of cows sashaying down the narrow lane, sometimes bumping into the hedge, sometimes each other, a collie nipping at their heels and the farmer patiently mooching behind. It was an enchanting sce-ne but Clare's thoughts were on darker landscapes. 'Could she really leave Simon?' her foot started tapping 'Could she really leave Grace to his viciousness? What would Bethany do? Her tongue was as sha-rp as her dads, she was so precocious and she seemed to have no respect or understanding about her mum's position. But she was her daughter and she loved her.'

Clare took some deep breaths of the damp air that was blowing strai-ght into her face and tried to focus on the calm lumbering backs of the cows. There was a row of swallows lined up on the telegraph wire, instinctively facing south. Soon it would be time to go. Would it soon be her time to go? She could hear an argument downstairs, Rosie was certainly holding her own but it was as if the words were being fired up the stairs straight at her. She had been trying to tell Simon that she was leaving but still had no idea what he planned to do. So far he seemed to ignore her but if he did start to believe it, she knew it could be more than unpleasant, it could be dangerous. Clare felt her blood pressure rise as her body scaled up into fight or flight mode, images of Simon's aggression and her placating, the kids in the next room at home. At these times sadness would overcome her followed by a feeling of helplessness. For always, her thoughts had been 'where could she go, who would be willing to harbour her, what about the kids, what would she do for money? How would she tell him?' The endless circle and cycle of musings, round and round in her head.

Looking round the restful old room, the antique oak bed with its soft mattress and lilac linen bedding, Clare compared the old place to the new executive house in Nottinghamshire. It occurred to her for the first time that she had never been part of the decision making in their relationship. Simon told her he had put down a deposit on a house she didn't see until they moved in. Set in the centre of a new residential estate, the carpets, kitchen and bathroom were all chosen by the developers. All was cream or beige with white plastic doors and windows. The whole estate was either four or five bedroom executive homes, set in a gated community with the emphasis on security. CCTV cameras and tall metal railings enclosed these 'lucky few' families. The gardens were a tiny square of communal lawn, a few shrubs running along the railings, two gravelled spaces for cars and a barbecue for each home. Clare would have preferred a tree. Very expensive, very luxurious, all the same, sterile and boring. And Clare hated it. Inside it was worse. The cream dining room hosted a huge, ostentatious table made from an unrecognizable wood with a gold leaf design around the top. A cream leather sofa faced a TV the size of a small cinema screen, an unused chess set filled a small table next to a drinks cabinet and fancy bar. The only pictures in the house were above the false fireplace and they made Clare cringe self consciously. They were huge photos of herself and Simon dressed up to go to a ball then Bethany and Niall as tiny babies. They seemed so conceited to her. But then, the whole house, the whole estate, spoke of tasteless conceit. The second lounge, a vast space, held one laz-y-boy chair facing another huge screen, a giant ceramic giraffe with bowed head watching from its corner and a giant golden monkey holding a silver tray, ready to serve its master, beside the chair. The sixteenth century oak dresser filled with the antique linens that Clare had collected over the years was banished to the tiny study along with her impressive collection of books. The old grandmother clock given to her as a wedding present sat silent in the corner, its filigree hands long ago stopped, covering the Victorian village scene behind them. Simon had said its chime woke him in the night. Yet the house was filled with electronic buzzers, pings and alarms going off at all times of the night and day. Reminders of heating, hot water, engagements and phone calls and that this was Simon's house, she was only there through his good grace.

As one of the other co-habitants in this luxury prison, Grace resided in a granny flat round the back of the house. Clare spent most of her days in this hot, airless place, tending the old soul. Neither of them spoke to many other people, just the postie or the odd delivery driver. The whole estate was like an empty desert, all the executives were at work, slaving away in offices through long hours to pay for their privilege they rarely inhabited. Birds and other wildlife had no wish to be there. Exotic cats, dangerous predators to any wildlife that dared to hang around this place, lethargically wandered the streets and there was very little food to be had amongst the barren shrubbery. The toads, newts, rabbits, badgers and foxes that had inhabited the woods, ponds and fields all dug out for the building of Oakwood View estate, (an ironic title), had long since fled or died.

Then there was the brain numbing boredom. It robbed her of confidence, purpose and energy.Conversations with her mother in law were repetitive attempts to persuade her to take the blood pressure tablets she seemed to consider an act of poisoning. The same with the healthy meals put in front of her nose just as Grace popped the last square of milk chocolate in her mouth and declared she wasn't hungry. There were the daily disputes over clothes, television programmes or radio stations. Nothing seemed to please Grace. Her whole day was a cycle of gossip, resentment or complaints. The few minutes that Clare had to herself were increasingly spent staring out of a window, vacuum roaring beside her or dish mop in hand, recalling the busy, fulfilling days of nursing. Although changing bedpans or taking the temperatures of elderly, complaining patients could only be thought of as mundane, she knew she was valued. Conversations with staff were good natured and fun and the reward of a wage made her feel useful and independent rather than trapped and sad. Yet still she had no idea how capable and well liked she was on the wards. Patients and co workers confided in this cheerful and empathetic nurse. The note on her leaving bouquet asked her to keep in touch and come back as soon as she could. No-one could understand why she left, never to be heard from again.

Abruptly, a little warm body landed on Clare's knee and curled, purring in her lap. It was as if the cat had sensed her misery. Distractedly stroking the soft fur calmed Clare's jangled thoughts and a more positive sense overcame her. 'She could do this. She would do this. She would leave Simon and take Niall with her. She would move to a village perhaps, Niall seemed to love the countryside as much as she did. Once again the decision was made. She would move into the countryside and make her life her own.'

In the next bedroom John, back from the pub, was staring up at the ceiling from the comfort of the bed. It was luxurious compared to his hard bed, lumpy pillows and sagging mattress at home. His flat was cramped with a mismatch of cast down furniture and cheap paintings. His one pride and joy, a photograph he had taken of an American aircraft carrier took up one wall. The one decent piece, a mahogany sideboard Grace had given him, was covered in dust and old Drs appointments, bills and demands from solicitors. Inside it was filled with the same. An old pressure cooker sat next to a lard filled chip pan and a cheap set of pans, bought on offer at Woolworths many years ago languished unused in the kitchen unit. John ate at the pub most days, Thursday was fish and chip supper for all the residents, otherwise he made sandwiches. Every so often council workers would paint his smokey, yellow walls or replace the greasy kitchen units but John would complain that they disrupted his day. The flat harboured a musty, mousy odour of old ashtrays, unwashed flesh and full bins. But John didn't care. It drove his elderly neighbours crazy but no-one dare say anything about the loud tele, the pungent smell that barged around in the corridor or the constant requests at their doors for a bit of sugar, a few tea bags, a cup of wash powder or even a fiver.

John watched cigar smoke twirl towards the open window, wondering whether he could be bothered to get up to have one final look for the bottle of vodka that seemed to have gone missing from the bottom of the wardrobe. Surely it wouldn't be those kids? And Simon and Rosie were arguing again, just like when they were kids. He shut his eyes and started to drift.

After another damp wander round the garden Dan was in the kitchen desperately trying to sketch the pub/workshop he had envisioned then drafted earlier before it drifted out of his mind. Now he was actually putting a plan together he realized the reality of how ambitious it was and the doubts set in. 'How arrogant to think men would listen to him. And how would he distinguish abusive men from respectful blokes who thought it sounded a great idea to have a pint and learn something about relationships at the same time. He would have to think the programme through very carefully.' Dan stared at the gentle sea lapping emerald rocks on his screen saver, scratched his chin stubble then sipped his tea and shut his eyes.

In the conservatory, Sapphire was now stretched out on the floor, her notebook open in front of her. She liked this room, the way shafts of sunlight played around the windows or the rain tapped out its tune , making her feel as if she were in a steamy rain forest. Since they had been here these elements had helped her creativity, she was pleased with the new songs stored in the notebook. She was trying to estimate the ages of her audience that evening so she could put together some kind of programme. She thought it would probably consist of older men, traditions die hard in country towns.

'Dear Universe, please not Elvis' she mused but she jotted down the titles of a couple of Elvis ballads, just in case. She would throw in some of her own compositions, just to see how they would be received, then a couple of Classics for Grace. 'I am not doing Rule Britannia no matter how often she asks for it. Aah but then Jerusalem is a beautiful song and I do so love William Blake. She'll be happy with that. And there's a piano in that big bar.' So Sapphy braided pastel dreadlocks through her hair and put on Doc's, black jeans and a pink granddad shirt.

Afterwards, she spent the rest of the afternoon daydreaming, staring out at the rabbits nipping out from the bushes onto the lawn. She was thinking back to when her love of protest music was ignited. A London street, packed with people slowly marching down the middle, all chanting, banners fluttering in the breeze 'Stop the War'. The amazing sight of the crazy, dancing steel bands. The conductor in black tail coat, white gloves, skilfully twirling his baton while walking backwards. Then the steel drums, young women in vivid tutus, pink, green or purple hair, ripped tee shirts and Doc Martens all dancing, drumming and watching the conductor. And this music, this amazing sound, beating out the rhythm of life, a cacophony of joy. As they passed, Sapphire watched, speechless. It was then she vowed to combine her environmental passions with her love of music. She would learn the drums and join a steel band, she had learnt the guitar and been in several bands. She would write protest songs then take them to audiences. Her thoughts went to her parents and the encouragement she had always got from them, the respect she felt for them. Then, her first boyfriend, her stomach did a loop as she pictured him, blonde, tanned, he could have been a Californian beach dream but he was a hippy from Leeds. Her mum took her to a contraceptive clinic the day after Sapphire took him home. No fuss, no lectures. She had remembered how it felt to be in a sixteen year old body. What an amazing summer in Cornwall that had been.

Her first guitar. She had worked in that dreadful cafe with its dubious hygiene practice and a bully of a manager. It paid lousy too, so it took ages to save enough to buy the scratched purple guitar off her cousin but it had been worth it. Then there were the other musicians she used to jam with in the upstairs room of her local, drinking coke and shivering with cold. When other young women were screaming at boy bands Sapphire was learning their trade and their secrets – be fearless, work hard and follow your talents.

'Don't you ever worry about being on the streets late in the dark?' her mother had once said, the only time she had revealed her fears for her daughter. Not once had she stopped Sapphire from travelling, dancing or joining groups. 'Why do you think I wear Docs?' Sapphy had responded. And that was that.

Sapphire turned onto her back and closed her eyes.

Grace, meanwhile, had woken up and crept off to indulge in her secret pleasure in the small study at the back of the house. She locked the door behind her, switched on the T.V. just in time to see Columbo driving his old French car to his latest murder enquiry. She settled down with her bag of mints and propped her feet up on the coffee table with relish. How handsome Columbo was, with his sleepy eye, his flop of black hair and brilliant mind. And those beautiful locations, manor size houses with outside swimming pools in the constant sunshine, far away from her cramped rooms at the back of a modern house in the middle of a dismal, grey country. No handsome male company to flirt with, just a daughter in law fussing about what clothes she should wear and what food she should eat. And she would constantly ask whether she had taken her tablets, it all made her feel so old and she hated being old. There was so much she still wanted to do, find a man who would take her away on those beautiful cruises they advertised on tele to start with.

Grace lost focus on how the murderer was covering his trail, her face started to sag and her mind wandered. She had an enquiring mind, she could have been a detective or a scientist and certainly a concert pianist, she thought, but then laughed at the idea of a woman detective - or scientist. For a moment she saw the audience on their feet, clapping her younger self in a floor length blue dress sparkling with sequins as she smiled and bowed. Then she was back in the room, in her old body, her wrinkled skin and sad mind. 'It's no good feeling sorry for yourself' she thought, 'Just get on with it.' And Grace forced herself to concentrate on the detective standing over a dead body and talking to the murderer beside him.

Celia had snuck off to the old shed to hide her scrapbook. She loved it in there and was glad the lads were playing together so she could have some time to herself. They got on really well and she noted how Niall's self confidence was growing daily now he was able to be young and mischievous. But they would not understand her 'She shed project'. Although Celia was full of mischief she also had a soulful side.

She felt very grounded and Celtic, had an empathy towards wild animals and loved ritual. She also felt part of nature and the elements, the rain on her face or swimming in a lake, the sensation of hot sand beneath her as she lay on a beach, the cold shock of running into the sea, waves parting round her sun hot body. Or the silent majesty of trees as she wandered down woodland paths. She noticed everything that nature showed her in all her seasons and weathers. Celia opened a box, more of her collections. She began fastening twine around the walls near the ceiling with drawing pins. Then, she attached feathers, shells, cones and stones from the beach to the twine, where they swung and danced in the draught. Draping a purple velvet cloth she had 'borrowed' from among Sapphire's festival items over a crate, Celia created a display. A delicate skull of a crow, a hunk of moonstone to represent earth, a dish of blue dyed rain to represent water, a black candle for fire and a feather for air. Then, covering Sapphire's tatty old sleeping bag with a pink Welsh blanket she had found in the cupboard, she laid herself down and began to read her new book 'The Pagan Goddesses'.

Suddenly, a cacophony of clanging rang through the house. Everyone jumped, the cat leapt off the bed, the dog scuttled under the table and the lads ran back into the lounge. Rosie and Simon were silenced mid-sentence. 'What the hell is that?' They looked round in alarm.

Dan raced in. "It's a smoke alarm. I think its in one of the bedrooms."

"John." Simon and Rosie shouted in unison, argument forgotten, they rushed up the stairs. A thin veil of smoke was hanging in the corridor.

Clare came out of her room, saw them, then saw the smoke and screamed. They dashed into John's room where another circle of smoke hung over the bed. The alarm above the door was still clattering but John was fast asleep, utterly unaware. 'Or was he unconscious?' Rosie fretted.

"John. Wake up." Rosie shook him and there was a loud snore. "You've scorched these bedclothes. Look at this eiderdown." she batted at a round black hole on the old eiderdown with her hand. The cigar, still burning, rolled off the bed and onto the carpet.

"You fool. You could have set the house on fire." Simon shouted as he picked up the cigar and threw it out of the window.

A sudden ringing woke Grace up, causing her to swallow her mint and, with a fearful old heart, she shuffled out of the room, calling for Clare. 'Where was everyone?' She slowly lumbered up the stairs towards the shrill noise, Sapphire right behind her. Celia and Bethany were the only ones not to hear the alarm as Celia was out of earshot and Bethany was half unconscious, sleeping off the rest of John's bo-ttle of vodka.

Meanwhile, John had opened his eyes. "I was having a lovely dream."he whispered groggily. I was just fetching the brand new black Jag I'd ordered after winning the lottery. Thanks for waking me up."

"You could have burnt to a crisp driving off in your new Jag, be glad we came up." Rosie retorted.

"A bit of smoke." John responded.

Dan bent and fingered the hole in the carpet. "This is still smoulde-ring. Will you stop smoking in the house."

"This probably means we'll lose our deposits." Rosie told him.

Grace appeared in the doorway, she looked groggy and was out of breath. "What's going on?"

"John tried to burn the house down." Rosie was deadpan.

"No need to exaggerate sis." Simon as always, defending his brother, despite yelling at him just a minute earlier.

John knew he had to win his audience over, stop them blaming him, making him look a fool. Everyone was hanging round the bed, staring down at him and unbidden tears were sliding down his face. Remorse was a new emotion to John. Stuff like this had never bothered him before and he couldn't understand it. Why was he feeling guilt over a hole in an eiderdown and why did it suddenly matter that the family were upset with him?

"I'm sorry." he mumbled into the pillow and Rosie stared, then leant over and hugged him. "It's OK. It's only a small hole lovey." She had grabbed the side of the bed in shock.

Clare also quickly responded. "It's alright John. Don't be upset. We probably over reacted but we were worried about you, that's all."

John looked embarrassed."I don't want to be like this anymore."

The two women glanced at each other. "Wow." Rosie mouthed.

"What's John on about?" Grace pushed her way to his bedside and looked down on her son.

He was rescued by the cat, fur bristling, leaping into the room, the grinning dog loping in pursuit. Abruptly, the cat whirled round and now he was Edward Scissor Hand, facing the dog, who slid to a stop and yelped as a claw rasped across her nose. In the confusion John crept out of bed and slid into the bathroom.

She had taken some persuading, but Grace agreed to accompany the Morris family to the pub to hear Sapphy's concert when excuses of tiredness and no outfit suitable for sitting in a pub just made them more insistent. She felt she was being most gracious by acquiescing and the family fussed around her in seeming gratitude. They knew really that Grace felt it beneath her dignity to be sat in a drinking establishment. Nor was she particularly interested in encouraging Sapphire's talents, after all no-one bothered with hers. Rosie had to escort her to the bedroom, admire several fussy, mother of the bride type outfits, help apply her brown make up and face powder, blue eyeshadow and red lipstick then try to comb through her blue rinsed, rollered and lacquered hair. All with a smile of encouragement rather than the sneer at her mother's snobbery as Grace's tone changed from rough Nottingham to the Midshires and she transformed from a fashionable, older woman to a sad Miss Faversham. Once she was ready she dismissed Rosie with a wave of her hand and the excuse she needed to catch up with the weeks' news then settled down on the bed and, hidden behind the broadsheet, she promptly fell fast asleep, smudging her lipstick and flattening her bouffant.

At seven everyone congregated in the hallway. They had all made an effort and dressed up for 'Sapphy's gig' as Ewan called it.

"You lot had better behave and keep quiet tonight." Dan warned the youngsters lined up by the door. "And don't go saying 'As if'. I know you lot of old, especially you Celia."

In the background Grace was already complaining about being tired and old and not wanting a late night.

"You haven't even left yet." Rosie responded in exasperation.

And when she heard the intention was for them all to walk down the lane to the pub she flatly refused.

"I'll take her in the car" said Simon in his no arguments voice. Really he didn't want to walk either, despite the pub being less than half a mile away. So the family set off down the tree lined lane, diamonds of rain droplets sparkling on the leaves overhead and dusk turning the hills to a blue mist. The sun was low on the horizon, rays stretching like gold fingers towards them as if pleading for a stay on this day's demise. The sky was lively with birds swooping into the trees to roost and cows were filing across the field after being milked. A mischievous breeze played with their hair as the two families pulled their jackets around them and loudly wandered in pairs towards the town, Sapphy confidently leading the way, guitar slung over her shoulder and shadows crossing her face. Only once did they have to step into the hedge as the Audi sailed by, the old lady doing her Queenly wave from the front seat.

Surprisingly the noise from within the old pub suggested it was packed. Summer events had finished and the townsfolk were glad to have some entertainment now the nights were drawing in. There was of course, an element of curiosity too. A young woman playing guitar and singing on her own, with enough of a repertoire to play for two hours. They didn't think so! The older folk were anticipating a bad performance they could criticize throughout the evening. A yellow beam of light thrust out of the open front door and welcomed the entourage through the darkness. Suddenly Sapphy stopped beneath the swinging 'Nags Head' sign, causing Ewan and Celia to crash into her.

"I don't think I can do this." she stated, her confidence hurrying back up the lane. "Look at all of them"

"Of course you can." Celia said, matter of factly. "Give me your guitar. I'll lead the way."

They squeezed past people in the corridor. Someone shouted "The singer's here."

"I feel sick."Sapphy whispered but she was pushed along by the tide of people behind her, passing John, flushed faced at the bar, until she found herself in the lounge, her family and locals shuffling behind. There were loud calls for drinks, Celia thrust the guitar into her sister's hands and, with a "You'll be fine" rushed to speak to Uncle John. Rosie and Dan followed to the bar.

Celia whirled around and rustled her dad's hair. "Can I have a cider dad?"

You'll get us thrown out, you will. You know you can't have a cider."

Two men propping up the bar wearing denim jeans, check shirts and flat caps glanced up from their beers to look at Celia.

"We do get local lads sneaking in here." the older one said. "But I don't think she'll get away with it."

Rosie wondered if that was due to Celia's age or gender. "She'll be happy with a coke." she smiled.

"You're not locals are you?" the younger man stood up and Dan braced to push closer to Rosie but both men smiled and moved away from the bar so she could move in and order. "Where are you staying then?"

Dan relaxed. "We're up at Cloud cottage."

"Now that's an interesting place." The man took the drinks off Rosie and passed them over Dan's head to the table behind.

"What makes you say that?" Dan asked, intrigued.

"Oh, not in a bad way. It seems a lot of good stuff happens there." The older man took off his cap, ran rough hands through silvery unruly hair and plopped his cap back on. Blimey, how many of you are there?" The young farmer was still passing drinks over.

Rosie, looking flushed and happy, was suddenly back beside Dan. "That's the last one." she indicated Grace's gin and tonic. "And two beers for you guys. It was so noisy at the bar I'm afraid I couldn't get your attention to see what you wanted." The men smiled and nodded their appreciation, Rosie continued. "Yeah, there's quite a family of us. Our daughter's playing tonight."

"Oh, it's your girl, is it? She's got quite a good turn out." The young man flicked a glance round the packed room and the two bar staff trying to serve a small crowd at the bar. "I think there's quite a bit of curiosity."

"I'm sure she won't disappoint." Rosie couldn't keep the pride out of her voice.

"You've not heard her play for three years." Dan teased.

"He's not with you, is he?" the older farmer shook his head towards John talking to two bored looking fellows.

"Afraid so."

"Oh sorry." the man looked chagrined.

"Let me guess. He trapped you at the bar, bored you to death, then tried to get you to buy his pint."

"You know him well."

"He's my brother." she laughed. "On that, we'd better go in and see if she's all hooked up ready to play. Not that we'd have a clue how to sort her electrics out.

The farmers followed and the bar emptied as people fell in behind.

Sapphy had been chatting with the nearest onlookers as she set up her amps and this calmed her nerves but they leapt up again as she saw the crowd filing in behind her parents.

Dan hurried over and gave her a hug. "You'll be fine."

The audience settled down at the tables as the bar staff lit candles and dimmed the lights, creating an immediate warm, glowing atmosphere. The singer was glad to see groups of young people, smiling and friendly among the older, more skeptical faces.

"Let's start with a song I'm sure we all know, should we? From a group I'm sure the youngest and oldest among us will have heard of."

She gave a glance round and quickly looked down to her guitar, her lip wobbling with fear. She struck a chord and began to play 'While

My Guitar Gently Weeps' by the Beatles. Immediately mouths dropped open and the audience became silent. Her voice was gentle yet powerful and the guitar became a harp, no, a violin and yet, a rock guitar, its passion filling the room. Sapphire sang through her repertoire, nerves cast adrift now. For the youngsters she sang 'Run' by Snow Patrol, complete with a Northern accent and they swayed to it, eyes closed. Then 'Purple Rain' by Prince, 'China Girl' by David Bowie, 'High Hopes' by Pink Floyd.Sometimes she moved over to the piano, guitar slung over her shoulder and then she would check on her audience. The whole room was smiling back at her, old and young, her family at first looked stunned but then sang loudly and joyously along with her, drinks held aloft. She had everyone's attention.

The young singer was also thrilled to see the audience remained attentive and smiling when she tried out her own compositions on them, slotted in between the favourites, even though they couldn't sing along, their feet were tapping and bodies swaying. 'Jerusalem' went down a storm. To this everyone stood up and sang at the top of their voices, young and old. Even Grace struggled out of her chair, grinning in disbelief. Sapphire's voice rose and fell in perfect pitch to the beloved tune. She then, somehow moved into 'Running Up That Hill' effortlessly, the audience running along with her. It could have been Kate Bush there in that country pub in the Lakes.

By the time she had done a third encore with a rousing 'We are the Champions', everyone on their feet, singing and swaying along, Sapphy's hair was wet through with sweat and she was almost staggering. Two and a half hours had flown by, Dan and Rosie had tears of joy and pride streaming down their faces, everyone was cheering and Ewan kept shouting 'That's my sister'. Only John and Simon were huddled in the bar, drinking steadily and muttering belligerent criticisms together.

Another half an hour was gone before Rosie and Dan were able to get near their daughter with half a lager carried over their heads like a prize. Her new fans, old and young, finally moved away after buying up all her C.D.s and assuring her 'she would go far'. Sapphy looked hot and exhausted yet her eyes were sparkling and she was talking excitedly, though hoarse. One by one her family lined up for a hug, especially Grace, who held onto her granddaughter's arm to escort her proudly out of the pub, talking about every song, the entourage following behind.

Once away from the porch light the darkness softly enfolded them and they all fell into a contented silence, each one thinking of the evening, Sapphy's voice, her guitar playing, her piano playing, her confidence in her performance, her talent! And seeking out her daughter's excited voice and laughter somewhere in the darkness, Rosie considered her a revolutionary, a role model for young women, positive, confident and capable, leaving fear of their abilities behind with the older generation.

Rosie looked up to the heavens, a mysterious midnight blue with its embroidery of silver stars and bewitching gold moon. She felt the chill breeze around her face, lifting her hair and then moving on into the black shapes of trees, causing moving spectral shadows across the lane. And she felt rooted in this ancient land, content and at peace with her life. Her daughter was a wonder. How had she managed to conceive this beautiful, musical and spirited being? Gentle Sapphire would be a beacon for young women and invite them to come alongside to be healed. Rosie turned to and smiled to see her daughters chatting to her mother, lighting up her sad life, giving her the attention she craved. The two boys were dancing around Dan, throwing wet leaves into his face and then running towards the ditch when he chased them, acting like he was going to throw them into the black gargling stream alongside. Then Rosie thought of Bethany sitting primly in the warmth of the car with John snoring in the back, agreeing with her dad when he wondered what all the fuss was about, it was just a bloody row as far as he was concerned and nobody knew about music like he did. But Rosie had seen that shadow of awe, curiosity and disbelief cross young Bethany's face in the pub lounge.

Tired now, the group hurried towards the welcoming lights of the cottage, promising warmth, hot drinks and comfortable beds.

Wednesday

Revelations

Dan suggested they all needed a bit of a break from each other after the angry and emotional exchanges over the last few days. Rosie had been telling Clare about a 1930's Arts and Crafts house nearby they could visit if she was interested. Although Clare was fascinated by the style and non conformist attitudes of the artists of the Arts and Craft movement, she knew that Simon would consider her going as insubordination and worried that Niall and Bethany would be the recipients of his wrath until he could turn on the real insurgent when she got back.

"Do you want to go to this house?" Rosie had asked.

"I'd love to go, but Simon?"

"To hell with Simon. Does he ever consider you when he fucks off to his golf or the pub? And, as usual, he and John have stepped away from the table leaving all the devastation. They've not once offered to help with a meal or clear up"

But Rosie had sensed the reason for Clare's hesitancy. She had a word with Dan and he agreed to take the boys sailing on Derwent Water. Niall was becoming less fearful about physical activities so happily joined Ewan running and whooping round the house when Dan suggested they should go canoeing. Celia heard them talking about a trip to Windermere and complained that she would much rather have fun on the lake than go on a rubbish bus ride to Windermere with boring Sapphire. There was even more tension when Rosie informed both Celia and Bethany that Bethany would be going with them, while casting a sympathetic eye towards Sapphire, who pursed her lips but made no comment. Celia at least felt more positive when Dan told them it was an open topped bus to the town, there was a witchcraft and book shop, plus he parted with cash to get a decent lunch. Bethany's objections became feeble when told staying at the cottage meant she would have to look after Grace. In a flurry of grabbing coats and bus timetables as the girls noisily left Rosie spotted Bethany smiling at something Sapphire was saying, then the front door slammed. Behind them went John, mooching down to the pub, a feeble wave as he passed the kitchen window where the women were clearing up the breakfast remnants. Dan and the lads were next, hurrying off before they were called in to help, grabbing bikes and noisily pedalling away with shouts of goodbye. When Clare asked what they were going to do with Grace, Rosie firmly told her to leave the rest of the clearing up to Simon and, as there was no golf, he could spend a few pleasant hours with his mother. She grinned, thrust Clare's handbag and jacket into her arms, pushed her into the conservatory, then called upstairs to Simon that everyone was going out and she hoped he would have a good day with his mother. Ignoring the angry calls coming down the stairs, with top notes above from the old lady, Rosie ushered Clare outside and slammed the door behind them.

"We're going to have a fantastic day," she assured as they drove down the misty lane.

"And soon you'll be having days out like this whenever you want."

Clare grabbed her sister in law's arms and breathed a 'thank you', then smiled, tears sparkling in her eyes.

"We'll support you. After tomorrow you'll be free. Don't lose heart now."

"No." Clare sat back against the old travelling rug that smelt of dog and thought how much happier she was in this tatty old van than in Simon's luxurious Audi.

. "I'm looking forward to today." she smiled. A soft tongue reached from behind and licked the tear off the side of her face.

"Sorry." Rosie looked guiltily across, "I've had to bring the dog. The girls would probably lose her and she'd capsize the boat if she went with Dan."

Clare laughed heartily. "It's fine, isn't it girl?"

"Just a quick walk then we can leave her in the van while we're looking round the house." Rosie assured her.

The old van chugged up the hills and dipped into the valleys, giving glimpses of the lakes between and Clare felt at peace.

Simon stood in the middle of the empty lounge and the silence filled his head. He thought that if the rest of them were going to leave mother then why should he bother. So he grabbed his newspapers and made his way up to the library for a bit of peace and quiet. Settling down in a squashy armchair looking out over the fields, he reassured himself that it would be good to have a day away from the stresses of work and his needy family. It was completely unfair of them all to just go out like that, expecting him to babysit the old woman. He settled back and dunked a biscuit in his coffee. 'Yes, this was the life.'

Downstairs in the conservatory, half concealed behind potted ferns, Grace was casting on her knitting. Sapphire had given her several balls of chunky turquoise wool she had bought in Keswick, along with the needles and pattern for a roomy cardigan. 'There gran,' she had said. 'See what you can do with that. I thought the colour would look lovely on you.' Grace was flattered, the least she could do was have a go at knitting it. Rosie had put Classic FM on for her and Clare had made a stack of sandwiches and a flask of coffee with a tot of Baileys in. As the sun passed through the glass it helped her old limbs unfurl and stretch. Grace decided she needed this time to think calmly and sensibly. As she cast on the wool an inner monologue began, almost as if there were two people in her head, arguing out the situation. The one, the frightened old lady who was screaming out for help in the only way she knew how, by moaning, blaming and feeling sorry for herself but never seeming to be heard. And now this new voice belonging to a braver, more open minded woman. This self had listened to Rosie, had acknowledged that she would be waiting till hell froze over for Simon to give her any attention and that only she could make her life happier by changing it. This voice also suggested it was not too late, she was not too old, that she deserved to get out of that toxic atmosphere. For Rosie had explained that Clare was going to be moving out, that her life was intolerable with Simon and she needed to break free. And wasn't it time for Grace to do the same? Time to stop complaining about how badly everyone treated her and admit that she was lonely and bored in that soulless house, just like Clare. Rosie then reminded her mum that a dear old friend had invited Grace to share her large house in the suburbs of Nottingham. Perhaps now was the time to consider it?

And as Grace began to knit, she reminisced over the wonderful times with Rosalyn when they were young mothers, striding proudly round the park pushing their coach built prams, awed at the joy of being new mums, sunshine on their faces, the delight of each other's company, of the War being over and the end of rationing.

So when Simon came down the stairs and with coat on, poked his head round the door and curtly asked if she wanted anything from the shops, he was nipping into Keswick, this lack of concern galvanized her decision to move in with Rosalyn if she could. So, while alternately staring out of the window and glancing nervously over her shoulder for any appearance of Simon, she had a long conversation with her friend on the old phone in the hall. Then she spent the rest of the afternoon planning after Rosalyn spoke of her own loneliness and assured Grace of her delight that her old friend wanted to move in. Her needles clacked and her mind whirled. There was so much to think about, so many questions for Rosalyn. By the time Grace had decided what furniture was hers by doing a memory scan of her rooms at home, she had finished the back of the cardigan. She felt an energy and enthusiasm not experienced for years. A carer and a cleaner visited Rosalyn every day and she assured that both would be happy to take care of Grace's needs too. She would have a sitting room to herself but they could eat together then spend the evenings watching T.V. or playing board games. Grace knew they would also spend a lot of time chatting and reminiscing and this is what she looked forward to the most. So when her old friend assured her that the rent would be so welcome in paying for many of the repairs on the ancient house she had never been able to afford, Grace was convinced.

The two sisters bickered and bantered their brisk sprint down the hill into Keswick. Bethany lagged behind, angry scowls masking her discomfort and a surprising new shyness . She was certainly used to being the centre of attention but usually as the school torment. Surrounded by a bunch of creeping cronies she would inflict spiteful put downs on the shy, unattractive or poorly dressed, laughing at their distress. This was happy laughter, taking in all their surroundings with the simple joy of life and it made Bethany feel mean. The girls unlocked arms to wait for her to catch up, then tucked their arms through hers and like a sunshine sandwich ran over the bridge to the bus station. Bethany experienced a bubbling elation that overwhelmed the ugly fiend living in her head. From its dark corner it remained in a submissive silence, so she found it hard to maintain the hostile eyes and spiteful, pursed lips.

The girls jumped on the wrong bus and nearly went to Coniston. Hustling off again and apologizing to the crowd trying to get on, they leapt back onto the pavement in time to see the Windermere open top bus about to leave. The driver opened the doors, Celia pushed them and in one noisy rush they chattered their way up the stairs to the front. The wind took their breath away as tree branches leaned in, leaves fluttering in their faces as they stood, dodging the branches while trying to keep their balance. They certainly had the attention of the other passengers but this was a grinning group giving their encouragement and Bethany couldn't help but grin back. When it drizzled with rain the girls ran to the rear of the bus and Celia put her umbrella up which, to their delight, kept blowing inside out. Huddled at the back the sisters became serious as Bethany spoke about her life in Nottingham. She recalled her teachers and friends with a smile that held no malice and hands that sat calmly on her lap.

The narrow pavements in Windermere were bustling with tourists, so frequently this caused the girls to step out onto the road. They shrieked as they pulled each other out of the path of a car.

"It's a good job my mum can't see this." Bethany breathed as Sapphy grabbed her arm to drag her back onto the pavement. The chattering voices all around and rainbow bunting crackling noisily in the wind caused even more confused excitement in the girl.

Snuggled between a gift shop, the window gloriously displaying stacks of pastel boxes of creams, lotions and soaps, and a bustling charity shop sat a tiny book shop. Stepping up the stone steps, beneath the porchway and through the ancient oak door, bell jangling above, into the dimness of the musky shop was like stepping back into Dicken's era. Sapphire spotted Celia's hand pointing to the doorway from midst a crowd ahead, then she disappeared inside.

"That's it. She'll be in her elements. You know what I think you'd love?" Sapphire took Bethany's arm. "There's a really good gallery just up the next street. Let's have a look round it, should we?"

Bethany's face clouded and the stubborn look was back. "Oh, I'm not really into that kind of thing. Aren't there any boutiques?"

"Just indulge me and we'll look at clothes after. I've seen some of your drawings. They're really good, you're clearly arty."

"Do you think?" Bethany's eyebrows shot up. "O.K."

They stopped by stone steps, a large single window above displaying a huge painting of a heaving grey sea in a storm.

"Here we are. A quick look round, then we'd better go fetch the bookworm and get some lunch then you can try on as many dresses as you want."

With Bethany lagging behind Sapphire hurried up the steps before her follower called out she wasn't going to bother.

Neither was the Arts and Crafts house a disappointment. Set on a hill, the views down to the valley were stunning. Low walls divided the garden into lawns, herb plots, shrubs and flower beds. Clare kept wandering outside to breathe in the tranquility between the view and the house. Twisted chimneys and mullioned windows clambered all around the Tudor brickwork. The smaller lawn hosted ornate metal tables and chairs with a brick path leading up to a Gothic door into the cafe.

"I'm hungry. Should we get something to eat?" Rosie was already heading up the path.

A few minutes later, balancing trays of sandwiches, coffee and cake, the two women headed for a table behind the low wall, protecting them from the wind but still maintaining the panoramic views over the fields, woods and hills. There was even the occasional silver glint of a distant lake when the sun slid briefly out from the clouds.

"I shouldn't be eating this." Clare eyed the huge slice of Victoria sponge as she plonked herself down. "It just called to me 'Eat me, I am delish!'

"Look!" Rosie pointed to her slice of chocolate cake and pulled a face. They both laughed but when Rosie glanced across the table her friend looked suddenly sad and serious, so she spoke up. "You know how, in the car Dan and I both said we would support you?" Clare nodded.

"Well, on our farm we have a small milking shed that's been converted into a living space. We've talked about this, Dan and I, so if you decide to leave you're more than welcome to live there until you find a place of your own. It's only small, we call it the Hobbit House but it does have a weeny kitchen, two bedrooms, a bathroom and a lounge.

Clare stared. Her eyes filled with tears. "I couldn't possibly."

"Why not? It's big enough for the three of you and, of course, you would be welcome to join us in the house for meals and chats, watch tele' or play board games with us.

"That,s very kind of you, I'd really like to, it sounds amazing but what about the kids?"

"You'd be doing it for the kids. Especially Niall. Think of the effect his father has on him."

"But the upheaval. They'd have to move school, that's if I could even persuade Bethany to come. She's such a wilful child, only does what she wants. I can't keep putting it down to teenage angst. I'm afraid she's spoilt." Clare's lip trembled. "They'd be leaving their friends. Anyway, he'd never let us go."

"You'll have to be strong, I know and we'll be behind you whatever you decide but you do seem to love the countryside..."

"I do."

"And there's a hospital in Exeter. It's not far, you'd be able to take up your beloved nursing again." Clare's face lit up, so, sensing attainment, Rosie hurried on. "Dan and I both said it would be fun, Ewan and Niall get on so well. We feel good about it."

Clare sat back and sipped her coffee. The birds sang in harmony. The world was full of possibilities. Her thoughts swirling, one minute alight with conviction, the next plummeting into a bog of impossibilities. Again she considered her city life. The traffic rumbling by the end of the road beyond the railings, the loneliness accentuated by the scurry of people hurrying past the high gates, off to work or rushing kids to school, dog walkers heading for the neat little park, a poor substitute for the wild nature she was experiencing in the Lakes. How her senses responded to the primordial smells and sight of the changing seasons. She stared out to the trees swaying in the distance. An east wind that returned scents of change and hope.

Then, abruptly, she remembered Grace. "What am I thinking? I can't just up and move sticks. What about his mother?"

"Let me tell you. I have already spoken to Grace. And she's thinking of moving in with her lifelong friend Rosalyn. You may have heard of her?" Clare nodded, stunned. "Anyway, its not like she treats you so well, is it? With her haughty attitude. She seems to think you're her maid."

Suddenly Clare grinned. "Bugger it. Yes. If you're sure and only if you will accept a rent from me, I would love to come and live in the Hobbit House in the Devon countryside."

Spontaneously the two women stood up and hugged.

"Now just the small matter of convincing the kids and telling Simon." Clare said ruefully.

"We'll sort out all the details with Dan later, after you've put your amazing proposal to the kids."

So, Clare's future resolved, they both settled down to eat their lunch.

Once inside the grand house it took a lot of concentration for Clare to study the antiques, the artifacts and ceramics made by the first residents of the house, exquisite as they were. When she looked up forlornly at Rosie after staring emptily at an emerald vase, her friend squeezed her hand.

"Don't worry there are plenty of old houses to visit up and down the country in the future. There's a National Trust stately home just fifteen minutes drive from our place!"

Tears slid down Clare's face, reflected in a spotlight but they were tears of gratitude not sorrow.

The journey back to the cottage was companionable and quiet. They only stopped for a brisk walk along a logging track in a pine wood, dusk dimming the treetops, the gloom and sudden cold causing the women to shiver and pull scarves over their shoulders. Released, the dog barked as she ran chasing squirrels. Rosie constantly whistled her as she charged into the brambles, worried she might disappear into the darkening woods. They were both glad to get back to the comforting old van and head back to the house with the promise of a good meal and stories of the kids' adventures. Clare shrugged off the uneasy thoughts of Simon's mood by stroking and flattening Celt's topknot till it was completely flat and the dog stared at her with reproach.

Back at the cottage, Rosie felt most encouraged when she opened the kitchen door. Dan and the boys had got back first and were in the throes of creating a huge shepherds pie. Niall had never cooked before but seemed to be enjoying learning this new skill, mashing potato with such gusto it was shooting out of the bowl and flicking onto the wall.

"A little less enthusiasm please young man." Dan laughed. "Or we'll have no topping to put on our shepherd."

Rosie blew a kiss towards Dan and crept away, silently shutting the kitchen door behind her.

"We don't even have to do dinner tonight. The lads are doing it."

"Is Niall in there?" Clare sounded amazed.

"Yes. Let us creep into the library and just chill till we're called for dinner. Mother's probably having her nap." said Rosie. Clare glanced guiltily up the stairs but all was quiet and she really didn't want to bump into Simon. He could be in a foul mood if he'd been at the beck and call of his mother all day.

The women settled behind their books, old wool travelling rugs around their shoulders to keep out the chill sneaking in between the leaded panes and rattling the windows. Clare kept staring up at the dusty rows of old books all around them on imposing shelves. She would take all her books when she moved out of the soulless palace and one day, when she had bought her own cottage, she would make one room a library, with an open fire and creaking old tables and sofas, just like this one. And this cheered her, she found it impossible to read, her mind kept showing short films of the final countdown with Simon as they were all leaving, then moving further ahead to her little home set in the garden behind the farmhouse in Devon. The new, amazing window on the world, Google, took her on a surprising virtual tour round the brick yard, the rustic wooden barns, a vegetable plot behind leading to a walled flower garden and pastures beyond. The farmhouse interior was spacious and airy and, most evocative, some windows revealed views of the sea only five miles away. The camera did not go inside her 'Hobbit House' but Clare was happy for the internal viewing to be left as a surprise for when she arrived. She thrilled at the thought of Niall's delight once he arrived at his country home, next door to the cousin he got on with so well. But her heart was mournful when she wondered about Bethany.

The latch on the front door of Cloud cottage occasionally rattled and voices could be heard in the lobby , a draught blew under their door as people arrived back, but the women remained undisturbed until Niall's voice resounded from the lounge, calling them all to dinner.

Chatting, everyone moved into the dining room, where the table was set and the lads were buzzing busily to and fro from the kitchen. Rosie had vowed not to instigate any arguments this meal time, so when Grace came downstairs alone, looking unkempt, she said nothing.

Even when they were all sat round the table and Niall bore in the shepherds pie as if it were a crown on a cushion and Simon's seat was empty, still she kept her own counsel. They were waiting for pudding by the time the front door latch rattled and Simon strode in to sit down with a curt 'Hello'. So hastily, before Dan could challenge him about leaving his mother in the house on her own, Rosie tried distraction by telling them the story of being fired from her first job.

"Don't think I ever told you about when I got fired from my first job, did I? There were surprised, then interested looks and she had her audience. "I was taking calls for a well known leisure park. Booking guests into the chalets and taking their payments over the phone. When one family asked to cancel due to their mother passing away and another family wanted to postpone till the next year as their daughter had broken her leg, I just refunded their payment obviously. As you would! But the company instructed me to go back and direct them to the small print - no refunds. I refused and they fired me there and then. It was only my second day." Rosie chuckled at the memory.

"I should think so." said Simon. "They're running a business not a charity."

"I thought they were heartless." Rosie added, ignoring her brother.

"I've got a 'getting fired' story." said Sapphire. Dan and Rosie pricked their ears up. "Oh yes?"

"Remember when you got me that job working in your friend's cafe mum?"

"Oh- Oh! Yes."

"Do you recall I didn't want to go that first day? That was because there was a music concert in Cornwall I was desperate to go to but I still wanted the job. I persuaded a friend to go in my place. I thought they'd never know but your boss checked in and my friend felt obliged to confess, seeing as they'd never seen her before. When I turned up the next day she fired me.. She did agree not to tell you though and I pretended to be going in the cafe for work until I started Uni."

"But that was weeks." Dan looked shocked.

"I know, sorry. If it's any consolation, the concert was brilliant, well worth it."

Rosie and Dan both tutted but before they had time to respond to Sapphire's confession, Celia, now encouraged, got something of her own off her chest.

"You know how I had that paper round?"

"Oh no, not another one." Dan groaned.

Rosie nodded dumbly, she began to wish she had never started the whole getting fired conversation. She had only done it as a distraction.

"On day two they were picking a girls football team at school. You know how desperate I was to get on the squad ?" Celia hesitated, glancing at her parents. "I got Jake Silvers to do my paper round for me."

"Oh no." Dan responded. "Mr unreliable."

"He was the only one who'd do it. It cost me three quid and all he did was stuff the papers behind a bush on Mr Bulcote's property. I got fired on day three."

"Let's not hear anymore." Dan insisted, taking a gulp of wine but Grace was getting into the spirit of the thing.

"Your generation's not the only one that can misbehave you know." She chuckled as an image came into her mind. "When I was nineteen I was working at Griffin and Spalding department store."

"Are you sure you want to tell us this mother?" Simon interrupted but Grace ignored him, lost in her own pleasant reverie.

"I was on the lingerie counter when a gorgeous American came in.

We chatted and I just sort of wandered away from my station and followed him through the revolving doors and straight to a very posh hotel where we indulged in some glorious afternoon delight." Grace's face softened. " I got fired the next day."

"Well, thank you for that." Simon muttered.

"Too much information, mother." John agreed.

Celia and the boys were nudging each other under the table and sniggering.

"Should we leave it at that for today?" Clare suggested and amid the children's laughing objections, the adults all agreed, except John, who had a quiet announcement of his own.

"I got fired from the Raleigh but I'm not going to tell you what for." and he would say no more. He could not resist the suggestion that he too, could misbehave. As if the collective group were not already well aware of this fact.

"He was nicking bikes." Rosie whispered to Dan. "He used to take the parts out the factory and put them together at home, then sell the bikes through newspaper ads. He has no idea I know."

"What's that mum?" Ewan was trying to read his mother's lips.

"I'm pleased to tell you that I have never been fired from a job." Simon said in a superior tone. I've had to fire a few myself though, reactionary trouble makers that they were. If they got jobs at all again bet they were as Union reps."

"I guess that's because you had your own company most of your working life." Clare rebutted. "And I'm not sure if there weren't some shady goings on there." she added quietly.

Rosie drew in a breath and glanced to see her brother's reaction. Grace started twisting her hankie and Clare appeared shocked at her own nerve.

"Can we just get these coffees doled out." Dan quickly changed the subject. " Who's hidden the chocolates?" The family all began to shout out where the chocolates might be hidden and the subject was finally dropped.

"We've had an amazing time." Sapphire called out over arguments over the chocolates, it seemed everyone wanted the hazelnut whirls. "Even moaning Celia, who loved the open top bus by the way. Branches kept banging against the window. You should have seen her laughing when one came over the top of the window and hooked the woolly hat off the woman's head in front of us, it's probably still hanging in the tree now. She bought three books then had no lunch money of course. Bethany very kindly subsidized so we didn't have to eat with her sad sack face watching our every mouthful."

Clare glanced at her daughter in amazement and Bethany, after first scowling, grinned with pleasure, her face pink at the acknowledgment of her good deed.

Sapphire nodded towards her. "And this young woman has discovered her career path. Why don't you tell them about it Bethany?"

Bethany looked round at her audience. The sullen face was back, her voice flat but her eyes danced. It was hard to disguise the exuberance after glimpsing her possible future. She didn't want this crowd to realize her new awareness though, it would mean acknowledging her bad behaviour and she wasn't yet ready for that. All the same she couldn't resist talking about the art she had been unaware of until she walked into that exhibition and the pictures leapt out at her as a beautiful, spiritual awakening.

"We visited an art gallery and there was an exhibition of artists called the Pre-Raphaelites. Oh, their paintings were amazing, so beautiful and so life like. The curator explained that loads of the everyday items like a glove or a handkerchief are symbolic. Like they represented an imminent death or the end of a love affair."

She clamped her mouth shut before it waywardly called out 'I want to be an artist.'

"I might know you lot would put fanciful ideas in her head." Simon stated. Bethany turned to frown at him, like his disapproval of her new dream was also an awakening.

But Clare gasped. She was speechless, all she could do was laugh with delight and run around to haul her daughter out of her chair to hug her. Bethany didn't respond, her arms hung limp at her side and her mouth was a firm line but her eyes still danced.

Later that evening, Rosie was trying to sneak a couple of hours of peace and quiet on the settee in the lounge with the company of the dog, a bar of chocolate and 'Juno', a film she had been wanting to see for a while. So, when Sapphire burst into the room, eyes flashing with excitement and calling 'Mum. Mum.' she tried to hide under a blanket. The girl was not to be deterred though and flung a large,red leather bound guest book onto her lap. "Look at this mum."

"Go away." was Rosie's response but Sapphire ignored her .

"You know what we've been saying about this cottage? Just read the entries in here." She straightened up and folded her arms like a smug school mistress who has just given marks of zero out of one hundred to an errant student.

"Really. Must I?" Rosie asked with a sigh as she fumbled for her glasses and read the first submission from the owners of Cloud Cottage.

Hello. We are the Wainscott-Turners and we have the good fortune of owning Cloud Cottage. We hope you have had a very comfortable and pleasant stay here and we thought you might be interested in learning more about the place. The house has been handed down to us through generations of my family. After investigating my ancestry it seemed that all who resided here documented their lives as being happy and content. They were simple, pastoral folk, mostly living off the land in harmony with nature. They have all passed down their wisdom around growing crops working with the seasons and weather.Many of these families also produced soaps, creams and cures from the herbs, trees and flowers from within this garden or the pastures around. Not only that, it seems a blessing to anyone who stayed within these walls was passed down from each scribe. In the early 1900's one considerate ancestor documented all these country crafts into one book. If you are interested, it is the green leather bound rather tatty volume on the bookshelf in the kitchen. Please feel free to take a browse and copy any of the information but please, please do not remove the book from the house. We feel it will bring bad luck but then, maybe we are just superstitious!

Please do read the comments families have put in this guest book and see if you agree that Cloud cottage is a very special place with magical powers. It would seem the inscription above the porch has come true for several visitors. Perhaps you? But again, maybe we are just superstitious!

"Have you seen the green volume?" Rosie looked sharply at her daughter.

Sapphire snorted. "You must be joking. Celia's got her mitts on it. You should have seen her face, it was a picture. Now she's dashed upstairs to that library room with it. We'll probably not get a look in, she'll be copying every bit down. What's really interesting is what other families have written. Just carry on reading, I'm going to fetch dad to have a look."

Like a storm passing through Sapphire ran out of the room again.

July 1985. The Singh family from Leicester.

There is something very special about this house! Not only have we had an amazing holiday but our asthmatic daughter stopped coughing and gasping for breath within three days of being here. The place is so peaceful and it was wonderful to see her breathing without effort. Being here enabled our decision to move to the coast or make our home here in the Lakes. Our humble and grateful thanks to Cloud Cottage.

August 1985. The Jones family from London.

We have had the most wonderful holiday and the effect of being in this place has been transformative. We arrived with a troubled son whose behaviour was on the verge of breaking the family up. He was disrespectful and sometimes violent at home but somehow the tranquility (or something) of this house calmed his black moods. The wonderful news is that a local farmer was asking at the pub for hands to help bring in the harvest and our son volunteered. I think he was as shocked as we were but he loved it! The physical hard work and fresh air turned him into a different person. It was like being here helped him to realize what would help him heal. Now he is going off to agricultural college and wants to become a sheep farmer. Thank you Cloud Cottage for turning our lives around.

July 1986. The Saville family. Suzy age 10.

Thank you. Thank you, house. My mum has been sad for so long. I used to blame myself for being noisy and lively. She would never talk about it but being here made her so calm and she talked to my dad about what made her unhappy. It wasn't me at all, it was something that happened when she was a kid. When we get home she's promised to see somebody who will help her mind get well. Oh, and I have had such a good time in the lovely garden, we don't have a garden at home. We are all so happy now.

Rosie put down her glasses, a bewildered look on her face. She turned as Sapphire and Dan came in the room.

"And I've only read some of the entries." she gestured helplessly.

"I know." Sapphire pulled Dan by the arm and passed him the book. "Read this dad."

"What now?" Dan sighed as he began to read.

"I've read them all, right up to 2000." Sapphire said. "There's loads of entries of people turning their lives around whilst here. I imagine the regular entries where people just say they've had a good time are people who don't need help."

Dan peered over the top of the manual, his eyes moist. "Remember the inscription above the porch? 'Enter these portals and find courage through love.' It seems so relevant, doesn't it?

"Let's see if Clare wants to add anything should we?" Rosie said with a grin.

"The magic of Cloud Cottage." Sapphire murmured and they nodded solemnly.

The heavy oak door creaked open and Celia bounced into the room, her face radiant as a rose at dusk.

"There's another book! It said so in the green one. It's purple leather." She could barely get the words out. "Where did you find the others Sapphire?"

"On that table by the front door."

The sisters rushed out of the room. A minute later they were back, Celia madly waving a notebook above her head.

"We've found it. It was in the book case in the hall. I bagsy reading it first, I found it."

"Fair enough but hurry up. I'll make some tea while we wait."

Still standing in the doorway, Celia started to read. It began with a potted history of the area. Though fascinating, for such feudal warfare to take place in such an area of natural majesty seemed inconceivable to the girl. Cumbria had been occupied by the Celts, the Romans and the Anglo Saxons. The original population dated back to the stone age and were responsible for Stonehenge and New grange Castlerigg stone circle. The Celts intermarried with the locals and settled but local families carried on feuding. The Roman conquest meant more bloodshed but civilizing habits too, such as bath houses and plumbing. It captured Celia's imagination to ponder the expanse of Hadrian's Wall, the intermingling of cultures and the interbreeding of Roman horses and native ponies, descendants of the hardy Fell ponies now grazing on the nearby hills. Christians fought Pagans, Kingdoms fought Kingdoms, families fought families and these brutal wars wreaked devastation on the towns, castles, monasteries and settlements along the borders. People living along these borders lived under the daily threat of robbery, arson, brutality and murder from all sides.

Celia imagined the horror and remembered the poems of Walter Scott. How the feuding between clans, governments and religions had been mythologized and romanticized. The communication even suggested that Tolkien may have based his fictional 'Lord of the Rings' and middle earth on the Cumbrian area, their Kings and tribes.

Then, on turning the page, in Gothic calligraphy the title ***'Our Descendants, the Witches.'*** leapt up in front of the girl's eyes. Her fingers tingled and stomach turned somersaults as the narration continued. She started to read out loud to a silent audience.

So, on dipping into our ancestry, we soon realized that the female lineage were primarily witches. At this point you may want to put this notebook down, thinking at the very least, superstitious nonsense and old wives tales. Or, at worst, ugly evil women who put curses on their neighbours and cooked babies. Unfortunately, throughout history, witches have been much maligned through religion and misogyny. Our ancestors were counsellors, midwives and herbalists, trusted and respected wise women of the village. Stories were passed down orally from mothers to daughters. Surnames were also passed down the female line so as to keep track of their genealogy. To the new order their offence was being old, female and Pagan.

Witches have lived in this house since it was built and some would say their magick has permeated the building, for it seems being within these walls solves the problems of families staying here. Whether that is true, or the benevolent atmosphere creates the right environment for people to solve problems themselves, I don't know. What I do wish is that people would not vilify witches so. If they looked beyond misogyny, beyond Christianity, they would probably discover our true intentions - to do good.

'Do No Harm.' *is our motto.*

Blessed Be,

Katherine Wainscott.'

Celia stared at the wall as if expecting generations of wise folk to be lurking there. She was remembering her mother's discourse at the dinner table and turned her gaze onto her. Rosie had read her mind.

"No. I did a course on feminism at university and witchcraft was on the curriculum. I am not a witch"

"Pity." Celia mumbled and wandered outside to check out the moon.

Thursday

Where's Clare?

Thursday began with a creeping grey dawn. There was no sign of the sun, just a gleam of pink beneath the constant gloom of rain clouds. The mountain mist billowed above the fields and hung over the house like a damp army blanket. In upstairs corridors toilets flushed, there was the shuffle of slippered feet, the dog sat up from her blanket midway on the stairs, grunted and sank back into sleep. The trips and activities of the last few days had finally exhausted the whole household and the cottage settled down again into silence apart from the occasional rattle of the old radiators and creak of rafters, punctuated with a sudden explosive snore. It was midday before the call of nature and need for tea provoked the stirring of people in each bedroom. The families waited, snug in their beds, for someone to go down and put the kettle on. It was Sapphire who stretched and sleepily staggered downstairs to make tea and breakfast. Ewan was close behind and was soon tasked with balancing steaming mugs of tea to take back up to each bedroom.

Clare opened her eyes and tried to ease her limbs off the chaise longue. She had slept surprisingly well, despite her legs being folded and neck bent throughout the night. She was dreading Simon's response to her unprecedented betrayal of wifely duties by not joining him in bed. But Simon had a cheerful smile on his face as he passed her, in fact he didn't acknowledge her at all, fixing his eyes on the bathroom. As the door clicked behind him, Clare immediately leapt up, grabbed her clothes and hurried into the hallway to knock on Rosie's door, her face a mixture of relief and tension.

Breakfast was peaceful, Simon even commented on the tastiness of the eggs, causing Rosie to scrutinize his face with suspicion and Clare to relax a little. Sapphire fussed around Grace, knowing she was going to ring her friend later to discuss the details of renting rooms in her house and would be anxious. As people cleared up and started to sort out the plans for the day there began an uneasy atmosphere as the showdown with Simon loomed closer. Neither had Bethany disclosed her intentions, she seemed unconcerned as she talked to friends on her phone, Clare tried to inconspicuously listen in but the talk was of clothes, boyfriends, the usual.

The lights were all on downstairs to cheer the drabness of the day and lift the despondent mood of kids aware of it being their last day at the cottage. They hung around in the lounge, switching on daytime tv and half heartedly opening puzzle books.

Celia was staring out at the cows huddled in a conversational group as if in an important meeting, her face impassive but her mind was chasing thoughts around, trying to corner them like the cows in the field. She was wondering why her mother always seemed to wind Uncle Simon up as soon as they were in the same room. It was true, he was unbearable but Rosie seemed to delight in picking challenging topics such as politics, feminism or the environment. As soon as he opened his mouth out would come beliefs polar opposite to her own. Was it her way of luring out Simon's conceit, to display it, like a steaming bowl of rotting fish for Clare to recognize how putrid the stink? Or were these challenges a vengeance for all the times Simon's spiteful tongue had tried to silence young Rosie while they were growing up?

Dan was busy working on his plans on the laptop and Rosie sat in the corner with Grace, trying to rework her knitting. When Clare went into the kitchen, Simon quickly followed and watched her fill the dishwasher.

"I saw something in Keswick yesterday that I knew would be perfect for you." he said, taking a small black box out of his pocket.

Clare was alarmed. "I don't want...." she began but Simon had thrust the gift into her hand.

"Go on. It's for you. I couldn't resist." He leapt across to open the box, revealing a jade star on a chain.

Clare was confused, there would often be a gift after an argument and she never knew how to respond. The necklace glowed against her skin as Simon fastened it round her neck. She could neither be as enthusiastic or appreciative as the gift deserved but neither could she refuse it. She knew that would engage his wrath and then there would be a lecture on how he knew he was rubbish sometimes but his work stressed him out, he loved her very much and only wanted to make her happy. But her intuition was ringing enormous warning bells in her head and she was learning to take heed of them. This felt like an appeasement, a bribe.

"I know things have been difficult for you." Simon smiled mildly, refuting any suggestion that it had anything to do with him, his hands resting on the back of her neck. "I thought we'd have a drive out to a lovely country pub I know of for a bit of lunch. Just the two of us, away from all this family madness."

Clare stepped back. "No. No. I can't.

"Come on Clare. What harm would it do? We'll just talk. I won't interfere with your decisions but we can't just go our separate ways in the morning without any kind of closure. We have to make some kind of plan. You owe me that."

Clare began to hear only sense in what her husband was promoting. She backed out of the kitchen, looking round the lounge for her allies but only Ewan and Celia were in there, playing chess. Her heart sank as she realized that Rosie and Dan were nipping into town to put petrol in the car and check the tyres, ready for the next day's homeward journey . All she could do was mutter 'Let me think about it' and flee upstairs. There, as if on cue, Bethany stepped out of her room in front of her.

"Are you and dad going out?" the girl asked, an unusual note of concern in her voice.

"I don't think so darling. You know how things are."

"I think you owe him that mum. He's so upset, he's just covering it up, you know, male pride."

Clare sighed, fetched her jacket and went down into the hallway, her thoughts agitated. Bethany sounded so sincere, it wouldn't hurt to talk it over with Simon, perhaps it was true, she owed him that. And then she must talk to Bethany, explain. She would disclose all that she had endured, all that she had hidden to protect her children. Bethany was old enough now to understand but was she too selfish, too much like her dad to empathize?

The girl watched from her upstairs window as her parents crunched across the gravel, her dad opened the car door, a benign smile as he guided her mum onto the seat, placing his hand on her head as she stooped. 'Like the police do when taking somebody into custody' she thought. Even from above, she could see the anxious look on Clare's face. 'She looks like she's going to the gallows.' Bethany whispered. In that moment her stomach lurched with fear for her mum. She even grabbed her trainers and ran downstairs, calling out that she would like to go with them but the car was already on the lane, a glimpse of white through the hedge, so she slunk back to her room, for once worried about someone other than herself. She had always sided with her dad, after all he was the one who bought her stuff and always told her mum to 'leave the girl alone'. Maybe her aunt's tirades had an effect after all because for the first time she recognized her mum's vulnerability and her dad's manipulation from that action at the car. Unbidden, tears mingled with her eye make up. She considered seeking out Niall to talk to him but pride prevailed. Her family were going to be split up in the morning and suddenly Bethany saw her own collusion in her dad's behaviour, causing her to experience new emotions of guilt and shame. Suddenly, all of her more recent vicious actions marched across her mind's eye. Her nastiness to her friend, her stupidity at agreeing to meet a stranger, the way she spoke to her mum and her arrogance in front of the other family. Her face contorted, it felt too much to bear. She desperately needed to talk to someone, so she sought out the sound of a guitar echoing around the house and sobbing, followed it to the conservatory.

In an old town of pastel stone houses, a couple are huddled around an old pine table in a garden centre cafe, surrounded by dark green foliage and white statuesque lilies. Wooden crates crammed with delicate herbs throw their culinary scents through the french windows and into the green gloom only penetrated by the golden light of church candles. Statues of angels and cherubs continue the theme of an ethereal sanctuary, while hop vines busily wind their way up the walls and across the ceiling. Clare is staring around, enchanted, hardly hearing Simon's suggestion that after their coffee she should pick as many herb plants as would fit in their car. That he would build several wooden containers for them when they got home.

"We could make our kitchen look like this." He smiled, folding Clare's hand within his. She was alarmed, again felt lost for words but dare not pull her hand out from under his, there were several other dim figures murmuring at tables nearby and she didn't want him to get cross. Simon had been attentive the whole drive, so she kept silent, tried to relax in the ambient atmosphere of this natural oasis and not give him any reasons for a scene. Yet she recognized there was safe-ty amongst these ghostly shapes and soon she would be alone with him in the car on the way to the pub. And here he was talking about when they got home as if she had never mentioned leaving him. So Clare refused the herb plants, and once back in the car, interrupted Simon as he proposed to move her bookcase and dresser into the smaller lounge so that her books would be more accessible. She even calmly regarded a row of horse chestnut trees forming an autumnal arch over the lane as the car sped among their shadows and Simon's expression darkened.

"Have you taken on board anything I've said?" Like the car gathering speed, she gathered a strength from deep in her belly, took a deep breath and looked directly at him.

"I'm sorry" she said firmly "But I am leaving. I am going to Devon. I've committed to move into the cottage on Rosie's farm." Then she sat back and waited.

Simon's frame seemed to expand, his hands now huge growths on the wheel. "Just answer me this Clare." his voice remained moderate. "Has your life with me been so bad?"

Clare knew she would be damned if she did and damned if she didn't! Still, she picked her words carefully.

"No. There have been good times. I just don't think we're suited." She turned her face away and concentrated on the structure of a Victo-rian bridge as they shot beneath.

"You realized that a bit late, didn't you? Seeing as we have two kids together."

"Leaving just didn't seem an option before."

"Before my meddling sister put ideas in your head, you mean." Simon was now scowling.

Clare hesitated, stopped to think what Rosie would say, immediately a red anger fired up through her body and like flames, the words spat out.

"No. Before. As in You really wanted kids but you were never home to be part of their lives, except to spoil them. Before. When You thought it would be a grand idea for me to leave a job I loved to look after your mother. Before. As in, You ran a business so You controlled the purse strings and made all the decisions. Before. As in You isolated me in a house I hated, away from my friends. Long before Rosie, Simon."

Clare knew she was on dangerous ground now but didn't seem able to stop. Simon's eyes were fixed straight ahead and the car gathered speed as the lane began to bend.

His voice was low and controlled. "You've been so hard done by, haven't you? A lovely home, two fantastic kids, you don't have to go out to work and an open cheque book to buy whatever your ungrateful heart desires. Now you think you're going to live in a shack on my sister's farm, do you?"

Clare stopped herself from glancing at the speedometer, staring at the bends ahead instead.

"Yes I do." she almost whispered, trying to sound calm, trying to keep upright, clinging to the seat belt as she was flung from side to side. With tyres shrieking the car dived around the bends, blind to oncoming cars or the hawthorn hedges leaning towards them. The grass verge, the trees, the cottages were all beginning to blur as they moved faster. She was beginning to feel dizzy and very scared but knew she must stay composed.

" And what about the kids?" he growled, glancing towards her.

"Niall wants to come with me. I don't know what Bethany's decided yet." She willed herself not to scream 'Slow down' as trees and banks loomed up alongside, almost seeming above them.

"You are not taking my kids." He yelled as they shot over the brow of a hill, the driver of an oncoming car flashing her headlights in alarm.

"Oh, so suddenly you care about them? You only seemed interested in spoiling them so they'd side with you."

Clare's voice competed with the shriek of the tyres now. She noted the raindrops on the windscreen gathering faster, fogging their vision and her stomach lurched. This could be her end. Just as hope had come into her life. This road, this weather, this man could be her demise this very moment.

"Simon, you may try to kill us both but I am not going to change my mind."

She had nothing to lose now. "I am not going back with you tomorrow and neither is Niall . I haven't been happy for years. You're impossible to live with." Hatred welled up through her body, her mouth was a thin line and her hands clenched into a fist around the seat belt.

"Hah." He grabbed her arm, the car swerved and brakes squealed. She shook his hand off. "I give you a year. You're nothing without me. You're fucking hopeless at anything. You can't make decisions. You can't even work a computer without me holding your hand."

"You'd never let me learn. I don't care how much you try to scare me, I'm going tomorrow."

He started laughing maniacally. "You want to go?"

"Yes."

Simon slammed his foot on the brake and the car skidded to a stop, swerving until it straddled the road, leaving black skid lines across its surface and the smell of rubber seeping in.

"O.K. Go. Get out." He leaned across and flung her door open. For a moment they both stared out at the lowering dusk, the empty lane, the rain loud on the tarmac and the hanging, soggy trees.

"But I can't. It's chucking it down."

"You should have thought of that. Get out."

"Simon, I don't even know where we are." Now one fear was being replaced by another but which was the more sinister she couldn't decide. "At least take me back to the cottage."

"Nope. Get out." Simon gave Clare's hip a huge push and unbalanced, she slid half off the seat, nearly falling into the kerb. Silently now she gathered her bag and coat and stepped into the storm, the wind immediately lifting her hair. The door slammed, again the tyres shrieked and with a fountain of rising gravel, the car snarled off, the driver neither checking his rear view for oncoming cars or glancing at the abandoned woman staring from the kerbside.

Clare's mind emptied as the rear lights disappeared. She knew not to think, that if she did, anger, fear and misery would overwhelm her. All she could do was physically feel the cold droplets hitting her face and a chill circling her shoulders as the grey intensified before her sight. Then the thoughts crowded. She needed to get out of the the road before a vehicle skimmed round the bend behind her. It was going to be alright. All she had to do was walk in the direction they had just driven. She was bound to see a car then she could stop it and get a lift. Clare dismissed the tiny fear around this logic. Common sense began to win the battle with panic. She refused to acknowledge that they had driven quite a few miles since the last village. Turning into the wind and pulling up her collar, Clare began to walk, for the first ten minutes rebuking herself for rushing out of the cottage and not first asking Bethany if she could borrow her mobile phone. She reminded herself that pigs would fly before Bethany would lend out her phone. Anyway, it was unlikely there would be any signal in this rural valley. Resolved, she wiped her wet face, stuck her hands in her coat pockets and leaned into the storm. Ahead, the trees were being flung back and forth, their black shadows swarming across her path like malevolent spectres. Twigs and leaves danced noisily in the gutters, while the rain whistled down her body. She felt compelled to step off the road and walk along the verge even though there were uneven tufts of grass, hidden holes and piles of dead leaves to trip over in the dusk. Clare pushed away the questions that swirled like the leaves and threatened to make her hurry over to the nearest tree and just wait for rescue. There were dangers that approached with the night, strangers stopping in cars or a car hitting her in the dark. Worse though, were the acknowledgments of Simon's cruelty in just dumping her, the thought of how much he must hate her. Now her anger forced her to march with determined speed and concentrate on looking forward to the hot soup once back at the cottage, her new jasmine bath soak , the satisfaction of telling the others how this final humiliation had strengthened her resolve to leave, her new life beginning the next day, then finally she willed herself to dwell on her future of love and support. She even chuckled to herself as she imagined the tirade Simon would get if he even dared to go back to the cottage. Now the sky had merged from lead grey into a gloomy black, making it hard for Clare to see ahead. Funereal clouds seemed to be marching towards her, each one larger, darker and more ominous. Silver rain streaks blew into her face, blurring her vision, dribbling down her chin and sliding inside the wool coat designed for cold not wet. Already her shoulders were weighed down and sodden. She cursed at her choice of fabric trainers, now heavy with water and rubbing at her toes. On this country lane, with no welcoming golden lights from house windows it could have been midnight rather than early evening.

Simon meanwhile, was back at the cottage. He parked on the lane, soundlessly lifted the heavy front door latch and tiptoed across the hall to the stairs in an attempt to go unnoticed up to his room, avoiding unwanted questions. But Dan stepped into the hallway in front of him.

"Hello Simon." He looked round. "Where's Clare."

"I don't know where she is, do I? She's not speaking to me." He glowered at Dan as he tried to sidestep past him.

"Yet Ewan and Niall both saw you going out in the car together." Dan smiled brightly.

"Well thanks to you lot, she told me she wanted to be on her own."

"Where was that?"

"On the way to the pub if you must know. I was taking her out to try and undo all the rubbish you two have filled her with."

Simon shrugged and headed for the stairs.

Clare had reached a crossroads and was desperately trying to recall their direction in the car. The village names on the dilapidated, wooden sign meant nothing so she headed for a huge oak tree at the junction and huddled under it. Her stomach had started to rumble and she pictured the family sat in the warm, eyeing up the steaming vegetable soup but hesitating to tuck in with her seat empty.

And sure enough, at the cottage Rosie had called everyone into the dining room. At the table they were all saying how sad they were to be leaving tomorrow and arguing about what they would miss the most.

"Never mind about that" Rosie angrily interrupted. "Where the hell is Clare?"

All eyes flickered towards Simon.

"How the hell do I know?"

"She went out with you." Dan sounded threatening.

"I told you. We were heading for the pub but she wanted to get out. 'To think things through' she said. She was going to make her own way back."

"She should be back by now then." Rosie said quietly.

The room went silent and everyone stared out at the black, storm tossed sky framed in the window.

Rosie leapt up. "You lot eat your soup. I'm going to see if I can find her."

"Rosie." Dan called but she had grabbed her coat and car keys and was gone.

Clare had randomly chosen the lane to her right and was now marching again. Amongst her unease, Clare's senses had begun to respond to the wild energy as noisy gusts played out their dramas around her. A picture of a memory of being a child and standing, wet through in a field, screaming with excitement into a storm, thunder yelling back and rain roaring in her face. She was fearless then, what had happened to her, how had she become so timid? Then she was no longer afraid so she lifted her arms and face up into the shower and laughed. She felt so alive, part of nature.

Suddenly, a strange sound on the other side of the hedge stopped her and the fear was back like an animal weight on her chest. Weakly she crept along a few more steps but the rhythmic sound followed. Not quite human but life of some kind or perhaps something that had once been alive. Still, she forced herself to retrace her steps and heart beating like a clock, tentatively parted the hawthorn and peered into the gloom. There was something white moving in there and it was making anguished noises. She sternly told herself there was no such thing as ghosts but all the same her legs turned to jelly so that she jumped back onto the road, then listened. Whatever it was, it was grunting in pain. Clare battled with the voice that told her to just get walking again and forced her way back into the sharp prickles.

As Rosie pulled into the pub car park and stepped into the porch the sound of laughter and conversation lifted her unease. 'Clare had probably got chatting and was enjoying her new freedom, for goodness sake, the woman deserved a bit of fun. Perhaps she'd join her with a gin and tonic before going back.' But as Rosie hurried between the bright faces in the main lounge, peered into the tiny snug interrupting a game of dominos, then into the bar and still no sign of Clare, her unease heightened into worry. She hurried back to the car, checking the loo on the way, just in case, then drove slowly back to the house staring out at the verges until her eyes ached.

The family were half heartedly eating their soup when Rosie stomped in and pulled off her boots, frowning absentmindedly.

"Any luck?" Dan asked, looking over her shoulder.

Simon had got up from the table and was heading for the stairs.

"Where is she Simon?" Rosie called over to his back.

He whirled round angrily. "I told you I don't know. She wanted to be dropped off."

"Where was that?" Rosie snarled.

"I don't know. Near some village, I just did what she asked."

"So, no names? No landmarks?" Dan joined in.

"Look. These lanes all look the same." he paused. "There was an old hump backed bridge."

"A bridge." Rosie snorted sarcastically. "Right. It's nine o' clock. I'm going to give it another half an hour, then I'm going to ring the police.

Simon tried to keep his expression calm. "That seems a bit..." But no one knew what it seemed as a blue light suddenly filled the window and the room fell silent as everyone stared out.

"Looks like there's no need to ring the police." John stated in his matter of fact way.

As one, the group raced to the door, just in time to see a policeman step out from behind the wheel of his car.

"Oh no. No.No. No." Rosie began a quiet moaning and Sapphire grabbed her hand. Only Simon stayed behind, trying to look nonchalant. Niall, Ewan and Celia rushed outside, then stopped, half blinded by the blue flashing light. Secretly, they were finding it all too exciting but their faces soon clouded when Grace, Sapphire and Rosie stumbled out, tightly holding each other, arms entwined. The policeman had gone to the back and was helping a bedraggled figure out of the car. No one moved as the two walked slowly towards them.

"Clare." Grace called in relief and, as one, the family stepped forward, as if a spell had been broken.

"What happened to you?" Rosie asked, as she hugged the shivering figure.

"I picked her up on the lane past Winchcombe's farm." the policeman told them.

Clare turned tired eyes to the policeman. "Thank you so much for bringing me home Brian." She took his hand. "And for the advice. I'll go to the solicitors first thing Monday morning." In one wobbly movement she hugged the solid figure. "Do you want to come in for a cuppa?"

"I'd better not, thank you Clare, I'm still on duty. But remember, if you need any help with anything, you've got my card." He turned to the others. "She's a very brave lass. She needs a hot meal and a bit of TLC." And with a few quiet words and a smile, Brian the kind policeman strode to his car, two young boys and a girl chasing after him, garbling questions at his back.

"Come on, let's get you out of this rain." Dan took Clare's arm and, as one, they all moved into the warmth of the cottage where Niall bent to tug off the waterlogged and ruined shoes and slid soft, warm slippers onto her red and scratched feet.

"Let's go into the bathroom and get these soaking clothes off you." Rosie urged. Then gasped as she spotted blood streaks down the filthy coat. "Where are you hurt Clare?"

"I'm not."

"But auntie, where were you going? What's happened?" Celia asked.

Clare stopped. A smile swept over her mud spattered face and she swept a dripping tendril of hair out of her eyes. Released twigs and leaves twirled down to the carpet. "You'll never guess what." Her audience gathered round, entranced. Simon, trying to escape up the stairs again, stopped, his back to the rest of them. "After thinking I was useless at everything," Clare continued, "Tonight I delivered a lamb." She straightened up her mud covered body with pride. They all laughed with delight, except Simon.

"Lambs aren't born in autumn." He said quietly, without turning round.

"Well this one was." Clare called angrily. "Are you calling me a liar?"

Rosie raised an eyebrow towards Dan. "So that blood is from the sheep?" she pointed at the ominous red streaks, then her voice sounded a new alarm.

"Look, you're blue. Come on into the bathroom to tell us, they can listen through the door." She shooed the group to one side and steered the unsteady woman to the bathroom.

So, as Rosie helped her strip off, mud, thorns and grass flying round the bathroom, Clare told of her adventures, not shirking from the row with Simon and being dumped in the middle of nowhere. Rosie rubbed her with warm towels while the bath was filling, as through chattering teeth, the adventurer told of being lost in the darkness. Then she checked the cuts and removed thorns from Clare's face and body as she described finding the sheep caught in the hedge, wool tangled in the thorns, distraught and struggling and starting to give birth. How it was so far into the thick tangle of hawthorn and privet it was easier to drag it, as best she could, through to the kerbside rather than climb over the gate in the dark to pull it into the field.

"I kept hoping a car or even better, a farmer in a Land Rover, would come by but it was such a lonely lane, there wasn't a soul. I never realized how strong and heavy sheep were." Clare tenderly touched her already bruising stomach where the sheep had kicked her. Rosie indicated the steaming bubbles and helped the exhausted hero into the bath, where she lay back with a sigh.

"What happened then?" Celia eagerly called through the door.

"Well, there were some complications with the birth which I won't go into and the sheep was certainly no help. It kept trying to get away from me. But between us, this gorgeous little lamb was born."

"Aarrhh." A collective sigh floated through the door.

"You should have seen it kids, it was all spindly with wobbly legs and black nose and feet. The mum accepted me then. I should think so, it was hard work." Clare giggled.

As she started to thaw out, energy restored, Clare was able to relay the rest of her eventful evening. She told them how hard it was to be a midwife, then sitting on the verge with the lamb on her knee, wondering what on earth to do next, the worried mum stood beside her. Then the police car coming round the corner spotting the strange trio and the relief when he stopped. Telling her story to a very kindly looking policeman who knew the owner of the sheep and rang the farmer. Minutes later, the sheep and lamb were safely in the back of a Land Rover ready to be taken to a warm birthing barn, the farmer gave Clare a big hug as a thank you and the kindly policeman brought her home. She told him how she had happened to be on that lonely lane in the dark and rain. He listened thoughtfully then gave her some advice.

Clare had not felt so cared for in a long time. The boys rushed off to fill two hot water bottles to put in her bed, while Celia and Sapphire hurried into the kitchen to warm up the soup. Bethany fetched her pyjamas and dressing gown from out of the airing cupboard and helped Rosie swaddle her now very pink mum in their warmth, giving her a tiny hug as she did. Even John fetched a tube of antiseptic cream for her cuts. As they all stood round the table, solicitously watching Clare greedily spoon down her soup, mopping it up with hunks of bread, they all agreed that Rosie should spend the night with her and that Simon should be informed by the collective adults that he would have to sleep on the settee in the lounge.

"That'll please him." John stated.

Eventually the lads went to bed, chatting with excitement. Rosie thrust a pillow and duvet in Simon's hands, which he accepted without a word and the tired families all headed up to their rooms. Clare was worried that Simon might come back upstairs, outraged at being shoved onto a settee and away from his wife, then demand that Rosie leave their bedroom, making a big fuss. So a bed was made up in Rosie and Dan's room, Simon was ignored when he protested and he crept off to the settee like a disgraced child.

Friday

Leaving

Clare had spent most of the night staring up through the darkness towards the patterns of light the wind shaken trees were etching on the ceiling of Rosie and Dan's bedroom. Ghostly leaves and branches swung around to a soft orchestral chorus of murmurs and gentle snores from the bed below. From her nest of duvets and eiderdowns on the floor, Clare turned her sore body and rearranged the bedding, knowing it was not discomfort that kept her aching eyes fixed on the shapes but her chattering thoughts. No sooner had she reassured one doubt than another niggled into her conscious. An image of her life at the farm, free from Simon's bullying and the boredom, living with a generous, loving family near the sea made her even more restless. She pictured herself cycling down narrow lanes with a swimsuit, towel and picnic or exploring the moors with Niall, feeding the chickens or cooking in the main kitchen while chatting to Rosie. But she could not picture Bethany in any of these scenarios. No more loneliness, no more guessing Simon and Graces' moods or trying to please their whims. Clare turned her head towards the darkened window at the lonely hoot of an owl and smiled. Tomorrow would be the start of her new life. She reflected on the cottage hospital just seven miles away from the farm, it would be so wonderful to go back to her beloved nursing. She just had the showdown with Simon to face first. Now though, outrage had shut down her fear, but then again the niggling. 'What was Bethany going to do?' Finally, exhaustion overcame her before that anxiety could get a grip.

As a watery morning sun shuffled into the room Rosie and Dan clambered soundlessly over the crumpled figure, prone on the makeshift bed. Without a word they passed their belongings over Clare's head, packed them into their dilapidated bags, tiptoed into the hallway and hauled down the stairs as Clare peacefully slept on.

Downstairs it was all action. Suitcases were being noisily trundled through the house. Ewan rattled by, sat astride his buckling transport, suitcase wheels squealing under the weight as Celia pulled it firmly by the handle. As one, Rosie and Dan headed into the kitchen, where they began spraying and scrubbing every surface, squabbling as they got in each other's way. Sapphire was frantically hurrying to empty the fridge ahead of them, calling out to the room in general, "Who brought the coffee, the tea, the tomato sauce, the olive oil?"

She had boxes lined up for each family.

"Oh just shove it all in a box for John." Rosie instructed, just as John rumbled past with a suitcase he'd acquired from Grace. He grinned with pleasure as he headed towards the garden.

"I should be helping." A disheveled Clare appeared in the doorway, a battered overnight bag from Rosie thrown over her shoulder, clothes spilling out the top.

"You were sleeping like a baby and we thought you needed it." Rosie said, still scrubbing. "You can tidy the lounge if you're looking for something to do."

As Clare vacuumed, her thoughts started spinning again. 'What a life changing holiday this had turned out to be.' Her bruised and scratched face was grim as she heard the banging of feet overhead. She knew the confrontation with Simon and Bethany was imminent. Would her daughter uproot and leave her home, friends and school behind or choose to stay with her dad? And now Grace was moving out to live with a friend. Simon was going to hit the roof. Clare plumped up the cushions with nervous vigour, worrying now about Grace, who normally relied on her to help dress. Trying to distract herself, she checked the cupboards and under the furniture for forgotten items, while chanting the mantra 'This too will pass.'

She lugged the vacuum back into the kitchen where Dan and Rosie were still cleaning. She could see John stretched out on a deckchair by the rose beds, a coat across his paunch, scanning yesterday's Daily Mirror, the customary cigar in his hand. The kids had been allotted jobs around the house and Clare could hear them laughing and complaining but Bethany's voice was not among them. Neither was there any sign of Grace or Simon.

Suddenly the door was flung open and Simon's bulk filled the frame. He didn't acknowledge anyone as grim faced, he pulled his case across the kitchen and straight out to his car. When he came back in Sapphire innocently asked if he wanted any of the food from John's box.

"No. I don't want any food." He exploded and thumped the door, making a fist shaped dent in the wood. Sapphire whistled softly through her teeth. 'Sorree.'

"What I want is for my wife to come home where she belongs, with me. What I want is my mother to come home where she belongs too, not drift off to stay with a 'so called' friend she hasn't even seen in years. What I want is an apology from you two for feeding them the rubbish that has instigated this ."

Then he waved his hand around the room as if the fault floated in the air. Rosie and Dan's heads appeared over the counter where they had been mopping the floor. Clare backed over to their side of the room then faced her husband.

"We've not been feeding Clare any rubbish." Rosie snarled. "We've supported her decision to leave you."

"You're aware then, that this is a private matter between my wife and I and nothing to do with you two dopes?" Simon was gripping the back of a chair and staring at 'his wife'.

"My decision is made Simon. As I told you yesterday. In fact yesterday's shenanigans makes me all the more determined." Clare forced herself to stare back, quickly removing her tremoring hand from off the vacuum.

"You can just unmake it and stop all this nonsense." his eyes glinted angrily. "You're coming home with me."

"No I am not. I'm going to live with Rosie and Dan in Devon."

"And what about Niall and Bethany? Have you ever given them a thought, without their mother?"

"I told you, Niall's coming with me." Clare took a step back.

Now Simon roared. "He is not. We are all going home together as a family"

Amidst the commotion no one had noticed Niall's slight figure appear in the room. He searched out his mother, ran across and laced his fingers through hers. "We are not going with you." speaking boldly he pulled up to his full height. “You’re a bully. Leave us alone.”

“I think you’ve got your answer.” Dan said calmly.

“And you can shut up, you pair of fucking trouble makers. Now get out to the car Clare. And you!” Simon moved towards his wife and son but Rosie was faster. She leapt forward, brandishing the wet mop at Simon’s face. “Get out of here. Now. Leave them alone. Or are we to ring Brian?”

Simon’s body stiffened, his face a livid mask. “Be careful where you’re shoving that mop.”

“And you be careful or I might shove this mop where the sun don’t shine.” Rosie twirled the strings in front of her brother so that droplets of scummy brown water flicked all over his scarlet face. In response Simon lunged for Clare but was blocked as the mop was thrust across his body. He managed to close his fingers around her arm.

“Rosie be careful.” Dan warned, he pushed forward to pounce and grab Simon’s elbow. Time stopped. There was an embarrassed silence as everyone waited, not knowing what to do next. It was this awkward scene that Grace walked into, asking what all the noise was about. She glanced at each motionless person and burst into tears. Suddenly John is at Dan’s side, firmly pulling Simon’s hand off Clare’s arm and calmly telling him to back off. The brawlers all turned to stare in astonishment at the brother who, a moment ago, had been sat in the garden quite unconcerned and was now looking steadfastly into the aggressor’s eyes. “I think you’d better leave.”

“All the times I’ve stood up for you.” Simon looked genuinely hurt. “You’re a-a traitor.” He was obviously lost for words.

The dog had wandered in and was glancing at each face in bemusement. Baffled, she looked on as Simon swung round and without another word stepped out of the French windows.

“Hang on, you’ve forgotten something.” Dan chased after him, picking up the cat basket, indignant bronze eyes glaring out and a banshee howl coming from its depths. He handed it over as Simon opened the car door.

Back in the kitchen a lively debate was going on. Clare was asking how on earth were they all going to fit in one van? Her tone was almost chirpy, relief transparent on her face. They all looked to Dan as he burst in with the dry comment 'Well that was fun.'

I bet the cat was howling wasn't he?"Clare asked. Dan nodded. "He'll do that all the way home." And they all grinned, breaking the tension.

"That'll drive him nuts." John said, then surprised them all by suggesting he take Sapphire and Celia to Penrith train station where they could find their way home by train. 'It will be a bit of an adventure.' he told the delighted girls. Then he would take Grace back with him to Nottingham and drop her off at her friend's house. When Rosie had recovered from the shock of John's hospitality she agreed that it would indeed be a great idea and with a gush of affection towards this reformed rogue, she rushed forward and hugged him tightly.

John staggered back. "Steady on sis." But he looked delighted. " What about Bethany? Where is she going? " he asked. "I can squeeze her in the back of my car if she's going back to Notts."

"And that is the multi million dollar question." Rosie stated.

"Where is Bethany?" Clare felt her stomach looping with anxiety. She needed to know, yet at the same time was dreading Bethany's decision. It would break her heart but if the girl wanted to live with her dad, she would have to accept it. Her thoughts were interrupted by Ewan smugly announcing he knew where Bethany was.

"I saw her heading for the shed."

Clare looked agitated. "Come with me, will you Rosie?"

The two women hurried down the brick path leading to the shed.

John and Sapphire were busy booking trains and Grace, for the first time, was making coffee for everyone when the little troupe meandered back up the path, mother and daughter holding hands, Bethany resting her head against Clare's shoulder, make up smudged and cheeks blotched from crying.

They burst in "Can we fit one more in the van?" Clare beamed.

"Of course." Dan laughed just as Grace struggled in with mugs of coffee wobbling on a tray. "I think we all need a drop of Baileys after that." she said, pouring generous lugs into the drinks. Dan looked alarmed.

"Not in mine Grace, I'm driving. And I'll need to keep my wits about me with this lot in the car."

Grace turned to face Clare, suddenly serious, her eyes full of tears and voice wobbly.

"I want you to know that I am not at all surprised you are leaving my son, I don't blame you at all, even I can't defend his behaviour. I was tired of hearing the snarling put downs and complete disregard for the other inmates of the house. Because yes, it was like a prison and I'll be glad to leave too, I took it out on you and I am truly sorry for that."

Clare hugged the woman who had once added to her misery, feeling the shaking old body through the silk blouse and could only say "It's alright."

The atmosphere was celebratory until Rosie remembered that in fifteen minutes time the owner of Cloud cottage was coming by to check for any damage and to give their deposits back.

"We have broken two glasses and a bowl. There's chocolate stuck on the lounge carpet and the burns in the eiderdown. We've got to put the plugs back on the stereo and radios. I don't know what Dan was thinking, I'm sure. Now there's that." And they all looked across at the fist shaped dent in the door."

"Oh dear." said Sapphire.

Rosie continued her list. " The shed window's broken, I have no idea how that happened but I bet I can guess who was responsible." She looked towards Celia who gazed innocently back.

"It was me, I'm afraid, Auntie Rosie." a teary Bethany confessed.

No one could understand why Clare was laughing and hugging her daughter with delight at this admission.

"What a week this has been." John looked sheepish, a new look for him. "Yeh, suddenly when he went for Clare I saw what a bully he was and how he always saw himself as superior. Then, in a flash I realized how selfish I was. I don't know, it was weird, the way it all suddenly came into my head." John shook his head, confused.

The children all nodded sagely at one another. "The magic of Cloud Cottage." Ewan whispered.

"You did surprise us." Dan said. "I always thought you were as thick as thieves with Simon."

"I thought I was too." John shook his head, baffled. "You know Rosie, I would really like to visit you before too long, I've never seen your smallholding." Rosie's jaw dropped. "I could bring mother with me if she'd like." He smiled towards Grace.

Grace positively sparkled. "I would like that very much my lad. We have a lot of catching up to do."

"You're not going to talk my head off all the way home, are you mother?" Then he grinned. "That's alright. So what if you do?"

And now everyone laughed.

Suddenly Clare looked serious. "So much has happened since we've been here. For me, it's like my life has unravelled and is now rewinding as it should."

"I feel so much calmer." Bethany said, squeezing her mum's hand.

"I feel so much happier." Niall added.

"And I feel so much naughtier." Celia danced around the united group, the dog at her heels.

"Oh no." Dan smacked his forehead.

"I definitely think it's this place." Ewan whispered to Niall as the family all squeezed through the conservatory to stand on the path. As one they formed a circle, grabbed hands and turned to look back at the house, the dog racing around them and barking with joy.

"The magic of Cloud cottage." Rosie murmured as they all stared up at the benign windows winking back at them like the eyes of a mischievous child.

"Should we book for next year then?" Dan asked with a twinkle.

"No!" they all shouted in unison as they hugged.